Dudley H. (Dudley Hughes) Davis

The Kingdom Gained

And other Poems

Dudley H. (Dudley Hughes) Davis

The Kingdom Gained
And other Poems

ISBN/EAN: 9783337171124

Printed in Europe, USA, Canada, Australia, Japan

Cover: Foto ©Andreas Hilbeck / pixelio.de

More available books at **www.hansebooks.com**

AND

OTHER POEMS.

By COL. DUDLEY H. DAVIS.

P. O.: QUIET DELL,

Harrison Co., W. Va.

RICHMOND, VA.:

B. F. Johnson Publishing Co., Publishers,

1896.

PREFACE.

WHEN the manuscript for my first book of poems was sent to the press, my mind was fully made up to write no more. But after the book was published and many of them sold, the solicitation of friends was so strong to continue to write that I was over-persuaded to do what I thought I had rightly decided not to do.

As I was not educated for a poet, and having spent thirty-two years of the best of my life in the mercantile business, I felt that it would be imposing on a generous public to write and publish another book.

But having disposed of nearly all of the first edition of a thousand books, and hoping that something better may be found in the next, I was led to undertake the great responsibility of coming before the public again with another book. If no one is benefited, then my work is lost. But if this book should please and benefit only a few, I should then feel that the unwritten blank left for me by this world will at least bear some traces of good ; and the highest hopes of your friend and servant will have been realized.

THE AUTHOR.

DEDICATION.

HON. LOYD LOWNDES,

Governor of the State of Maryland:

MY DEAR SIR:—We were school-boys together. And while I have lived a quiet home life, you have built your monument towering above the clouds of disputed fame, which will ever stand an honor to your native county and State.

Please allow me to dedicate this, my second book of poems, to you as a token of admiration for one of our own county and State.

I hope you will permit me, sir, to subscribe myself,

Your friend and servant,

D. H. DAVIS.

BIOGRAPHICAL.

THE subject of this sketch, DUDLEY HUGHES DAVIS, was born March 23, 1834, in Harrison county, Virginia, what is now Dodridge county, West Virginia. His early life was spent on a farm, and had but little advantage of educational privilege. His grandfather, William Davis, came from New Jersey, and was one of the first settlers of Harrison county. His father, William F. Davis, was a soldier in the war of 1812. At the close of the war he, William F. Davis, was married to Miss Rachael Hughes, whose parents came from the South. She was a cousin of "Hickory" Jackson. William F. Davis, after his marriage with Miss Hughes, settled in what is now Dodridge county, then a wilderness, where white man's foot scarcely ever trod before. There they raised a large family of children ; the author of this book of poems was one of the youngest. He left home at the age of twenty-two, and attended school at Clarksburg, at the old West Virginia academy. There he was a classmate with men who are now prominent business men ; among them is Judge Nathan Goff, and Loyd Lowndes, Governor of the State of Maryland. In the year of 1856 he left school and engaged in the mercantile business, near his father's home. In 1858 he was married to Miss Emily Rickard, his first love. He and his young wife then moved to Quiet Dell, a small village near Clarksburg, West Virginia, where he again engaged successfully in the mercantile business for thirty-two years, when he closed out his stock of goods and purchased a valuable farm on Elk Creek, between Clarksburg and

[7]

Quiet Dell, and like everything else he undertook, he knew no failure. He soon showed to his neighbors that if he was not an experienced farmer, he was at least a practical one. He was president of the first Board of Education of his district, and helped to put the free school system into operation. In the year 1876 he went into convention with a delegation of 100, and on the first ballot was nominated as a candidate for the Legislature, receiving eighty-four votes. But owing to an independent candidate was defeated by forty votes. In the late civil war he was commissioned lieutenant-colonel of his regiment. During all the toil and care of his business-life his mind was at work in the literary field, and he would think and write poetry; and why, he says, he cannot tell, except that a topic would present itself to his mind, and he could not get rid of it until he would write something on it. He never thought of publishing a book, and it was only through the solicitation of friends that he ever consented to have the first volume of his poems published. On the issue of his first volume he was the recipient of many compliments, among them were the following:

A friend from Jackson Centre, O., writes us as follows: "I have just received a copy of Colonel D. H. Davis's Poems, and find it full of rich gems of original thought. The Colonel has a true poetical nature." Written to the Editor of the *Telegram*, by Rev. J. L. Hoffman.

Another is from the *Baltimore Herald*, the paper he used to write poetry for: "This little book has met with favor from New York to California. Judges of the courts, prominent lawyers, clerks of moneyed institutions, prominent literary critics, etc., pronounce the little book a gem. It will live, and as a relic which time will not efface. It has the radiance of a golden sunset, whose hallowed glow will throw its beams athwart the shades of the valley, and the glitter anew on the shore eternal."

" The curious will find pleasure in reading his poems, and the cultivated and refined will be entertained by a perusal of this work."—*H. L. T.*

CLARKSBURG, W. VA., October 8th, 1893.

DEAR MR. DAVIS:—I have read with much pleasure your Book of Poems, and admire its originality and style. In fact I am so much pleased with it that I have bought one copy for each of my children, except one son, and want one for him and one for myself. Take the production all in all, it is an honor to you, and an honor to the State. Yours very truly,

B. WILSON.

And again under date of January 29th, 1896, Ex-congressman B. Wilson makes use of the following words at the close of his letter : " Your style is good, very good, but it is not the style that makes the book valuable ; it is the originality of the ideas and matter ; the force and beauty of the language by which they are expressed. Having had the book called to my attention by our correspondence yesterday, I re-read most of it last night with very great pleasure, indeed ; realizing new beauties that I did not catch before. It is a series of beautiful productions, chaste, instructive, attractive and elevating."

" It has been my privilege to read the manuscript of Col. Davis's new book, and find it full of high, moral and patriotic sentiments. I am sure it will be the means of bettering humanity where ever it goes."—*Rev. W. L. Burdick, Ph. B., D. B.*

CONTENTS.

[11]

ILLUSTRATIONS.

[15]

THE KINGDOM GAINED.

The Kingdom Gained.

As I climbed the hill of ages,
And finding the shades of life
Thickly falling around me,
And weary with the toil of many years,
I stopped to rest and to consider.
I was soon lost
In the mysteries of creation,
And the realities of Eternity,
And I fell asleep, and I dreamed a dream
Which was not all a dream.
And as the bright far away
Mysteriously spread before me,
The great mirror of life
Spread its silver wings
To the golden hills
Which were sun-tip'd by the love of youth;
I beheld a vast valley;
And it was called the valley of youth;
And in the midst thereof
Was a crystal river,
And it was called the river of bliss;
And I beheld many towns and cities
Spreading away from its shore,
And the bloom of youth
There, variegating with love and virtue,

2 [17]

Had its brightness and its charms
Indellibly stamped forever.
And the happy homes were blest
By loving eyes and ladies dear ;
But the most beautiful
And charming scene of all,
As a vast crowd stood in a hall,
And as the bright silken folds
Of the curtains fell away,
The fairest angel of earth
Robed in her own beauty
And with grand display
Appeared in her bridal robe ;
Ready to mingle her fortune of love
With the one who stood by her side.
Thus to join the great procession of life
Which was then on the march
Through the cloudless valley of youth.
And the sunshine of love
Dispersing the clouds of discord,
Cast a radiant gleam
To glitter anew on the shore eternal.
And the banks of the river of bliss
Were lined with small boats and canoes ;
And they had no sails,
But were driven by the arms of love.
And two came walking to the shore,
Buoyant with hope and confidential love.
And a vast multitude of friends

Were gathered together ;
And they stood beneath the shades
Of the wide-spreading trees,
And the parson stood in their midst,
And while yet as two, they were one.
And they walked the golden sands
Of the crystal river shore.
And they chartered a boat,
And their boat was lined with rich flowers,
And filled with gifts of rare beauty.
And they stepped therein ;
And on the side of their boat
In bright golden words it was written :
" It is not good for man to live alone."
And their boat had two oars—
One for the right side and one for the left ;
And the name of one was love,
And the name of the other hope.
When seated they moved from the shore,
Both lifting their oars at the same time,
And smoothly glided away,
And soon reached the shore of prosperity,
Where they sold their boat for a price,
As it had carried them safely across,
And the bright valley of prosperity,
In all its grandeur, spread before them.
And I saw two bright young men,
Who walked in great haste ;
And they unlocked their boat,

And on the side it was written:
"Gold is might."
And on both oars was written:
" To the valley of prosperity."
But both oars were for one side,
And as they pulled away
Their boat turned round and round,
And on the stream, still drifting down,
To lodge upon their native shore,
With their lop-sided boat
And two right-handed oars,
And their courage failed them.
Then came a beautiful young bride,
With her brave companion by her side;
And their boat was bright and strong,
Armed with two glittering oars ;
And they moved out in splendor,
And they run well for a time.
But, alas ! they did not pull together,
And their boat rocked as by a storm ;
First one way, then the other,
But still drifting down the stream,
To lodge upon the island of despair,
And to live in the cabin of poverty,
With the wolf of hunger at the door,
The lion of discord in the hall,
And the thistle of contention in the field,
And their flocks were shaggy and poor.
Then came an old man

And a beautiful young girl,
But they did not match;
And when they sat out,
Did not pull together,
And were disgusted with themselves,
And went back.
Then I looked away, away,
And I saw the belle of the town,
But far away from the shore;
And she was charmingly beautiful,
Courageous and faultless;
Too noble of heart and pure of mind
To accept stained offers.
And she wrote her banner
In bright letters of gold,
And she swung it to the heavens
And to the bright shore of bliss;
Gracefully came tripping along,
And on her bright banner of gold,
Written for all to behold.
And as it floated above her head
With the bright golden letters, she said:
"I'll paddle my own canoe."
And the pride of the young men
Followed her to the shore
And would gladly have gone with her;
But she feared to trust them.
And she chartered a long canoe
With only one seat, and one oar,

And pulled away from the shore.
But her oar being for one side
Was minus power the boat to guide :
And thus, she drifted on the sea.
And in vain applied the useless oar,
Still drifting on the sea of bliss,
To land again upon her native shore.
Then in the streets of the town
But near the river shore,
Came a tall handsome man
With his banner in his hand.
And thus it was written:
" I have sought a companion in vain."
And near the shore of the river of bliss,
He met the beautiful lady
Who had abandoned her canoe,
And who was on her return
To her friends, and native home.
And seeing the gentleman's banner,
She told him of her sad adventure,
And that no one could cross alone;
And that the term bliss applies
To no one who seeks it in disguise.
And thus she said, " the distant shore
Is never reached with single oar."
" My name is bachelor," he said.
My name or looks the ladies dread ;
Now as you have been on the sea
I pray thee, sweet maid, accompany me."

" For name or looks," the lady said,
" I'm sure, dear sir, I have no dread.
I'll forsake my banner and canoe,
And seek one wide enough for two."
He placed the ring upon her hand,
And then they left their native land.
Their boat was light and run with ease,
And drifted smooth upon the seas ;
And thus they found that one meant two,
And boat in place of long canoe.
Their home was near the gentle sea.
Where the beautiful valley
Spread its green fringy wings
To tip the foot-hills of the distant west.
There the fleecy clouds of eve,
Sat on their golden pillows ;
And cast their sun-tipped flash
O'er the green velvet plains,
And the towering, gray-walled peaks,
Which like crowned kings
Rose from the sweeping skirts
Of the distant trailing plains,
And which were bright walled
By the variegated hills
Of the fading east.
And I saw that the valley
Was blest with a happy people,
Not too poor to live,
Nor yet too rich to die,

And enjoyed the only true pleasure
Allotted to fallen man,
Which, robed in its true form,
Is religious contentment.
In fields of green, beyond the plains,
There shepherds camped by day and night ;
Their flocks increased, their fields made gains,
And years were lit by prospects bright.
And truly 'twas a prosperous vale,
And from the hills, when nights were long
And wolves were howling on the trail,
The shepherds blew their warning song.
As music from the trumpets fell
And blended with the distant bell
Which hung within the tall church spire,
It fell and blended with the choir.
And the churches also had their shepherds,
And they watched their flocks
By day and by night.
And they stood upon the watch-tower,
And they blew their mighty trumpets,
And the voice of their trumpets fell,
And they scattered the wolves of hell,
And forced the dragon to his den,
And cleared the thorny paths of men.
And the voice of their trumpets fell
And touched the chords of Heaven's bell,
Which, blending with the new-born soul,
Vibrating through the dome of gold.

And earth's converts in Heaven swung
The golden bells, while angels sung
And spread the news through all the skies,
Which rose from earth and mortal eyes.
And a lamb was slain,
And the shepherd marked his flock
With the blood of the lamb ;
And he had a book
With a golden seal,
Which was the seal of Heaven,
And his flocks were enrolled therein.
Then the dragon again appeared,
And he also had his flocks,
And they were marked with a mark,
But no one knew it but himself ;
And he sent some of his flock
To the good shepherd,
And asked to have their names enrolled.
And the shepherd knew not
What manner of men they were,
And he took their names.
And the dragon taught them
By what means to disturb the flock ;
And great contention arose,
And they knew not from whence it came ;
And the dragon's imps set about
To unveil the hidden fault,
And many of the shepherd's flock
Were accused of great fault,

And were sorely tried;
And then he accused others;
Then the shepherds brought him
Before the council.
And they found that he was
A wolf in sheep's clothing.
And the shepherds blew their trumpets
And the wolf sneaked away to his den.
Then the dragon appeared on the streets
In the form of a man,
And proclaimed to the world
That the shepherd and his flocks
Were no better than the wolf,
Or they would not have had him
As one of their flock.
Now the good shepherd
Called his flock together,
And they counseled among themselves
That they had driven the wolf
From their flock.
And they all rejoiced
With exceeding great joy,
And praised God for their deliverance.
The scene now became grand
Beyond all earthly paintings;
And I did not wish
To break the visionary chain
Which had lengthened out
Even beyond the stars.

And sweeping the vibrating chain
From the belfry of Heaven
Even to the sinful earth.
As the telephone of Heaven,
To waft the good news away
To the bright angels of the skies
And by which the soul of man
Might feel the vibrations of love
As it touched the wires of Heaven above.
These scenes came rushing fast
Full of brightness and great joy.
Then the valley of youth disappeared,
And again my eyes traveled
By the strange flash of dream,
And I saw the great valley
Of the middle age.
And it had no bounds :
But as did also the valley of youth,
Spread away from the silvery sunrise,
Even to the blushing clouds of sunset.
And in the midst of the valley
Was a bold and rushing river,
And it was called the river of gold ;
And it was fed by small lakes
And widespreading inland seas.
And a vast cataract broke the silence
Of the deep blue current
As it hurried down the rapids
To make its final leap,

From which there arose
The sound of muffled thunder,
And rainbow spray;
And which fell like silvery dewdrops
On the white foaming billows
Which rose and swiftly hurried away.
And as the vast river
Spread its blue arms away
By the lakes and the seas,
It held within its grasp,
All manner of ships:
Life-boats, war cruisers,
And pirate vessels.
And millions crowded their decks,
For it was called the river of gold;
And there came many
From the happy valley of youth,
Even forsaking friends and homes,
Risking life, forsaking liberty,
Defying heat, facing cold,
For the drifting sands of gold;
And millions rushed upon the shore,
Forsaking happy homes of ease,
For the golden pebbles of the seas;
Life was bartered, Heaven scorned,
Hell defied, honor sold,
For inventions to sweep
The glittering sands of gold.
And men gained vast millions;

Nor did they stop upon the shore—
Nay, millions called for millions more;
And spires of cities rose
Like clustering forest pine
Stripped of their towering green robes;
And the hum of spindles,
And the roar of steam,
And the clatter of cars,
And the buzz of saws,
And the rush of millions on the street,
Brought millions to the millions feet;
Yet brought not happiness nor ease,
But sent more ships upon the seas
To face the storm and risk the fall
Which plunged beneath the cataract wall,
From whence no ship has e'er returned.
No pleasure, then, upon the sea;
No pleasure, then, within the town;
The sons of wealth were never free,
But with the yoke of gold were bound;
Nor did they stop to loose the weight,
As crushing mints returned in gold;
But higher rose the flooding gate,
And adding speed to every mould.
And I saw that much wealth was a failure,
And that those who sought pleasure
In that direction,
Were only heaping coals of fire
Upon their own heads.

And the chain of the dragon was loosed,
And he went as a roaring lion
And spent much of his time
In trying to deceive the rich man
As to the amount of his wealth
And the worth of his soul.
And the churches went begging for bread,
While saloons were overflowing
With gold and wickedness.
Tall church spires rose to the skies,
But only as a monument
For Heaven, in mockery.
And the golden calf stood on the street,
And millions worshiped at its feet;
And the dragon set his mark
On many, very many;
Yet the true shepherds
Were faithful to their flocks,
And fought the wolves of the dragon
With the voice of their loud trumpets,
And set the seal upon all
Who would hear their voice.
But when gold and religion
Were placed in the balance,
Religion was found wanting.
So with all the grandeur
Of the beautiful city:
The dragon was king,
And worshiped by a vast

Majority of the people.
And I was greatly troubled,
And wished myself back
To the happy valley of youth.
Then my eyes took wings and flew away,
And I saw the rich valley of old age;
And it was only the rich fringe
Of the valley of youth,
And the valley of the middle age.
And in the midst of the valley,
Gently swept a beautiful river,
And it was called the river of care;
And on its beautiful shores,
Vast cities dotted the valley,
And glittering spires rose to the clouds,
And golden chandeliers
Lit the bright walls,
Of the churches and halls.
And all classes of people,
And all ages there dwelt,
And those who worshiped God
Were happy and content.
But from the great valley
Of the rich middle age
There came great ships,
Burthened with millions of gold,
All seeking safety
In the valley of old age,
And were sailing the river of care;

But pirates were on the sea,
And robbers were on the shores.
And at the homes of millionaires,
Beggars stood at the door;
And while their vast ships
Countless millions bore,
They feared to land upon the shore—
They feared to sail upon the sea.
And so the mighty chain of gold
Enslaved the men who once were free.
Slaves? Yes, cruel slaves;
Not slaves to a tyrant, or a king,
But slaves to the gold they bring
To imprison them
Within their steel-lined vaults;
To sip the bitter cup
Flowing from the river of care,
And eat the bread of constant dread.
And I saw that great wealth
Was also great slavery.
And that the happy days,
Were in the valley of youth,
Where the wealth of love
Was greater wealth
Than the wealth of millions.
And very many old people lived
In this paradise of earth;
And churches lined with gold
Told the story of the city.

And while their millions of gold
Enslaved many of the people,
Yet thousands more of the people
Obeyed the shepherd's call,
And had the stain of sin cancelled,
And had their robes cleansed
By the blood of the Lamb,
And had their names written
In the Book of Life,
And they bore the seal of heaven.
On the banks of the river of care,
A man of great age
Sat in the door of his vault,
And he wore the cloak of religion;
But it hung loose about him,
And did not seem to fit.
And he seemed restless and uneasy,
And a doctor passed that way
And he tarried with the old man,
And he talked with him quite a time.
And the doctor told him
That he must soon leave
The great city of care,
And find some other world.
And the old man became sad,
And very greatly alarmed;
And he sent for a shepherd,
And he told the shepherd
That he had worn the cloak

Of religion, even from
The distant valley of youth,
And all the way through
The many years in the
Prosperous valley of the middle age.
And that under the cloak of religion,
That he had been enabled
To gain very many millions;
But after coming to the
Religious valley of old age,
He had found that the cloak
Of religion did not fit him,
And therefore would be
Useless to him any further;
And that he had no seal nor pass
To the kingdom.
And he told the good shepherd
That he had vast millions
Of gold in his vault,
And that he would give it all to him
For a ticket to Heaven.
But the good shepherd told him
That all the gold in the world
Would not buy one ticket to Heaven;
But that he could get a ticket,
Without money and without price.
But the old man told him
That it was now too late,
That he must soon go;

And had not time to get a ticket,
Unless he could buy one.
The good shepherd told him
That there was none for sale,
And reluctantly bid him good bye.
And then the dragon appeared
In the form of a moralist ;
And with his smooth, silvery tongue,
He told the old man
That his course through life
Was all the pass he needed for Heaven ;
That he had been honest and upright,
That he had employed the poor,
And that he had fed the hungry;
And gave liberally to the church,
Sent missionaries abroad,
And had lived peaceably with all men ;
And for all these good deeds,
And upright life, he should be
Richly rewarded in Heaven.
And the old man became reconciled,
And put on his cloak of religion
Again, and went his way.
Then the good shepherds of the city
Stood upon their watch towers,
And blew their mighty trumpets ;
And the people of the city
Turned their eyes that way,
And thousands obeyed their call,

And had their names written
In the book bearing the golden seal,
And great joy prevailed in all the city,
And men of great wealth
Divided their gold with the churches.
And the shepherds flock grew to great numbers,
And the dragon became alarmed,
And he clothed his wolves in sheep's clothing,
And sent them among the shepherd's flock,
And even had their names enrolled
As they did in the valley of youth.
And some of them changed
The color of their wool,
And became as black sheep,
That the church might drive them out,
So that the dragon might accuse
The whole flock by them.
Others set a bad example
Before the bright young men,
By leading them away
To the saloons and card rooms ;
And argued that no harm
Could come from one glass,
Or a civil game.
But one glass led to another,
As did also one game lead to
Another game, and another glass ;
Then the wolves accused them,
And the churches drove them all away.

Then the dragon proclaimed
Through the mouths of Universalists,
That all men should be saved,
And that men of the churches
Were no better than other men.
So the higher the shepherds
Built the walls of the churches,
The higher the dragon
Built the fire against them.
But when the church was silent,
The dragon was also silent,
Hoping that the fire of the church
Might die out by not being stirred.
Then came two men, to the shepherd,
Who wore the wrinkles of many years,
And one of them said to the shepherd,
"What shall we do to be saved?"
And the shepherd said,
"Seek thy sins to be forgiven."
Then one of the men said,
'In the bright valley of youth,
I set out for the kingdom,
And for my journey.
I took the road of morality,
As I thought that was the true way.
I have followed it strictly,
With a bright hope of at last
Gaining the kingdom.
Most of the way I have traveled alone.

On my way I overtook this man,
Who said he was on his way
To the Kingdom of Heaven.
And we traveled a distance
On the same road.
But we at length came
To another road,
And it was called Universalism.
And we there enquired
The way to the kingdom.
And the gate-keeper told us,
Either road would lead us there,
But the road of universalism
Was the shortest and surest way ;
"For," said he, "it matters not what you do
You will get there by this way."
And I saw that my companion
Was not disposed to be strictly moral ;
And after a long debate
With the gate-keeper,
He left me and went that way.
And again I made my journey alone,
And on the way I met a man,
And again I enquired the way,
And he told me that I was wrong,
And that my road would lead
Me down to endless perdition.
Then doubts arose and I was troubled.
Then I stopped by the wayside,

And enquired again,
And the man at the gate
Assured me that I was safe,
So I went my way.
And behold I came to one asleep,
And when I stirred him,
I found he was my companion
Who had gone the other road.
And he told me that way
Led to the dragon's den,
And that the road morality
Ended at the same port.
And I believed it was true,
And we knew not where to go,
But hearing of the good people,
And of the good shepherds,
In the happy city of old age,
We set out together again.
And now we come to thee
With our lamps well nigh
Destitute of oil.
But while the wick of life
Still remains may we not have hope?
Yes, said the good Shepherd,
God bless you, hope is on your side;
You have been led away,
But the way to the kingdom
Is very plain and delightful;
Your lamps must now

Be filled with the oil of grace,
And your hearts filled with
The love of God,
And become new creatures
In Christ, who died to save sinners,
And you shall inherit eternal life,
And you shall be of my flock,
And go with us to the kingdom.
And they fell at his feet,
And prayed for mercy.
And the telephone wires of Heaven
Were again touched by
Their simple and earnest prayer,
And the answer of peace
Was felt in their souls,
And they were marked
By the blood of the Lamb.
And their names were written,
And they were sealed for the kingdom,
And great joy prevailed.
It now seemed that this was all a dream,
Yet I believe it to be true.
But as the wealth of this world
Was not what it seemed to be,
I was troubled, and tried to break
The deep slumber of my dream.
Just then, in a strange tone,
The voice of a fairy said,
"Not yet, not yet;

Thine eyes hath not seen,
Nor hast thou conceived
Of what yet lieth before thee."
Then the fairy took me away
To a towering sun-capped peak,
Even above the golden clouds
Which swept around its rugged walls.
And the fairy gave me a seat,
And it was gilded
With the rich gloss of sunshine,
And all around was very bright.
But as the bright, fleecy
Clouds swept away,
The sun closed its glittering wings,
And drop'd down into
The golden sea of the fading west.
Then the bright rays of the silvery morn,
And the starry chandelier of the heavens,
Drove the mist and darkness away,
Which had hung o'er the valley below me.
And lo! it was very bright.
And another valley then appeared,
And it was called the valley of death.
And in the midst thereof
Was a strange and beautiful river,
And it was called the river of Jordan;
And its waters were as white as frost;
And its sands as the sands of a desert,
And no life appeared in all the vale;

Then great fear came upon me,
And I prayed the fairy to take me away.
Then I looked as through a telescope,
And I beheld the three great valleys
Through which I had travelled,
And I saw that the life of man
Was but an inch of time ;
One inch only allotted him
To make preparations
For the world eternal.
Then the voice of the fairy said,
" The young hum-bird oils its wings,
Grows strong, and flies away.
But the one that stains its wings
From the sticky pool of tar
Will never, never fly.
The man who oils the wings of his soul
With grace of the living God,
Will grow strong in faith,
And when he sinks
Beneath the sea of death,
Will rise again with golden wings,
And, in the clouds, will fly away.
But the man who stains
The wings of his soul
With the tar of the world,
Shall rise from the sea of death
Robed in the pitch as full for the flame."
The fairy hung this painting

Before me and went away.
And I did not understand its words,
But became more reconciled;
And again turned
To the strange valley before me;
And while as yet no life appeared,
I beheld many paths, and roads,
All leading to the river of "Jordan";
And I saw no boats thereon,
And no paths leading from its shore;
And no turning point appeared,
While beyond the further shore,—
It was bright-walled, by
The eternal hills of the kingdom.
And I then saw that I stood
Between life and death.
And again great fear came upon me,
And I knew not how to go hence;
And I turned and looked back,
And I beheld a vast world of people,
And they all seemed to be drifting that way;
Not because they would,
But by the strong chords of nature,
And which bound each one fast;
And which coiled around
The great windlass of time,
And which could not for a moment check;
And all classes, rich and poor,
And all ages, moved in that direction.

And I saw a man of great age,
And he led on far before;
And behold! it was the old man
Who had left the valley of youth
By the road morality,
And who I had seen fall
At the Shepherd's feet
In the city of old age.
And then a lady appeared
In another path, but close by,
And she was from the rich valley
Of the middle age.
She was gracefully tall,
And very beautiful,
And wore a crimson silk.
And now they both neared
The great river of Jordan,
And I shuddered with fear;
And they both walked upon the sea;
And as they went began to sink
And fell away beneath the surface.
And again I trembled with fear,
But lo! they burst from the other shore
With brightness to dazzle the sun;
Both robed in gold, and angel wings,
And each a trumpet in their hands.
And a chariot cloud swept about their feet,
And they rode thereon.
And on the sides of the chariot,

In letters of flaming gold,
It was written:
"The Kingdom Gained."
  (*The above line gave this book its title.*)
And their chariot wheels
Rolled on the golden clouds of Heaven,
And as they swept away
The cloud, which hung before them,
Vanished before their brightness.
And then the bright walls
Of the Heavenly Kingdom appeared.
And as the two angels blew their trumpets
The great pearly gate
Swung on its golden hinges,
And two angels appeared at the gate
With two crowns and two harps,
And they met the chariot cloud,
And they bade the two angels come in ;
And they placed the crowns upon their heads
And the harp in their hands,
And left their trumpets outside the gate.
Then a voice, as by a trumpet, said:
"Well done, thou good and faithful servants,
Enter thou into the joys of thy Lord."
And a new song was sung ;
And the dome of the heavens rang
With glad tidings and great joy.
And the pearly gate swung to,
And the clouds of the heavens

Again hung o'er the city walls.
Now, after all this grandeur
And great glory, I then understood
The painting of the fairy.
Then I looked away in the valley
And I saw a beautiful lady
From the valley of old age!
And a step behind a small girl
From the valley of youth:
And as they went said not a word.
In another path came a man
From the banks of the river of care,
And he walked with a gold-head cane,
And had the cloak of religion
Thrown about him;
And behold it was the old man
Whom I had seen on the bank
Of the river of care;
Who sat in the door of his vault,
And talked with the doctor,
And who was persuaded
By the agent of the dragon,
And who again took for his pass
His cloak of religion,
And they all three sat foot on the sea,
About the same time,
But as they went fell away.
But quick as sunlight flash
They rose from the watery tomb,

The lady and beautiful girl,
With robes of righteousness,
Angel wings, and trumpets;
And the little girl had grown tall,
And wore a robe and had wings,
As did also the lady.
Then the chariot cloud
Swept them away,
And the vales of the heavens
Folded away before them;
And I watched them no further,
For the old man had also appeared,
And he was greatly changed,
But had no robe nor trumpet.
He watched the two angels,
And started that way;
But the golden cloud on which
The chariot wheels had rolled
Melted away before him,
And he turned away and came back.
And lo! he bore the marks of the dragon,
Which was a photograph of the
Dragon, on his forehead.
And he seemed to be sorely
And distressedly disappointed;
But at last turned away
And passed down the silent stream,
And was lost in the darkness
Of a dismal cloud,

Which spread away from the shore.
And then, as I looked again,
I saw a beautiful girl
From the valley of youth,
Representing the morning of life;
But as she neared the river shore
I saw her rosy cheeks
Had began to fade,
And her steps became slow,
As though weary and faint,
And she stopped not for the Jordan,
But passed on its bosom
And was lost as beneath it;
But with dazzling brightness
Burst from the other shore,
And was swept away in the golden cloud,—
And as the shrill voice of her trumpet rang
The veil of the heavens swung back
And the pearly gate stood ajar;
Then appeared the two angels, as before,
With their harp and their crown.
And then appeared another angel,
And he clasped her in his arms;
And behold it was the old man
Whom I had first seen lead the way;
And she called him father.
And in all her brightness and glory
She was not more beautiful than he;
And they passed beyond the gate.

THE PEARLY GATES.

I saw the crystal fountain
Which flows from the throne of God,
As it lifts its golden spray
In heavenly clouds,
To fall like dew drops
On the never-withering bloom of **Heaven**,
Which shall live forever and ever.
And as I looked again,
There was great commotion
Among all the people ;
And many were in the paths,
And many more on the roads.
Neither did any turn away,
But many reached the shore ;
Even many at the same time.
Many of whom flew away
In the bright golden chariot,
But woe be unto those who did not!
For I then saw the great dragon
Burst from the frosty white sea,
And he walked upon the water,
And he had seven heads,
And also seven horns :
And his horns were as shining brass,
And heads as the heads of serpents ;
And his eyes were as flaming fire,
And his dress as the scales of fish ;
But they glittered like shining metal,
And the water of the sea

4

Stood not on them.
And as he went he roared like a lion;
And his voice was that of distant thunder,
And flashes of lightning stood about him,
And those who had rose from the sea
Without trumpets and robes,
Turned them away,
As they feared to look upon him.
And as he turned to go hence,
On his back it was written with fire,
"Follow thou me:
For thou would'st love darkness rather than light
Because thy deeds are evil."
And his course lay down the stream,
And as he went many followed.
And then the great lane of hell appeared,
And on the finger-board it was written,
"Broad is the road."
And I saw it was hedged in
By rough towering walls on either side;
And at the further end was a gateway,
But there was no gate,
And on the black, charred arch above,
In sooty flames, appeared these words:
"Room for all."
And I shuddered to look again,
And strove to break the slumber of my dream;
But as I fell away again
I saw a rich man, who came

As though no fear fell across his mind.
And also came a beggar,
Who had begged at his door.
And they both rose with golden robes,
And trumpets alike in their hands.
And the poor man became as rich
And as bright as the rich man,
And on the chariot cloud stood equalized,
As up they rose to the world in the skies.
Nay was his millions of the land
Worth robe or trumpet in his hand?
Their chariot cloud, ten thousand fold
More valued than a world of gold.
Their chariot rolled on wheels of fire,
Ascending fast, ascending higher;
And sweeping to the golden gate,
Where crowns of glory for them wait.
My cup of joy was running o'er,
For brighter grew the heavenly shore;
And, as the myriads soared the skies,
'Twas then too much for dreaming eyes;
I then stepped down from out my dream,
And long, to me, long did it seem.
I'm sure 'twas long, but not in vain,
Should courage rise the crown to gain.
Or should it cause one sinner turn
This side the gate, where soot flames burn,
Or should it cause the sparks to rise
Which light the journey to the skies,

And stamps this painting on the mind,
To live for Heaven and things divine.
Could all my life be in the song,
I'm sure 'twould then be none too long.
This painting, drawn with brush of dream,
Brings me new thoughts of Jordan's stream;
For as we sink beneath its sting
We rise with harp and angel wing,
Or to the endless pit of hell,
Where spirits dam'd shall ever dwell.
And by this painting I now see
New glories of eternity
Half hidden by that golden cloud
Which o'er the walls of Heaven bow'd
Oh, yes, I see beyond the gate,
Where angels stand and gladly wait
To welcome, with a harp and crown,
And swell the millions circling 'round.
And now I see the golden hill
And valleys wide and widening still,
With drifting clouds of golden spray,
Time sweeping through eternal day,
While silvery mist-like dew-drops fall
Mingled with love, and love for all.
Now, as this was not all a dream,
But lost in the eternal theme,
I'll hang the painting on the wall,
Lest some might stumble and thus fall,
To rise upon the other shore;

As cast away to rise no more.
This painting shall grow brighter still,
To all who live and do God's will;
And when we step upon the sea
'Twill then reflect eternity,
With all the golden chandeliers,
And angel eyes with loving tears.
And all our friends upon the shore,
Who from our homes have gone before,
And as they sweep the golden strand
They'll welcome all with angel hand.
And through the bright eternal day
Sweep through the clouds of golden spray.
Now, as my dream and song is done,
I pray thee learn it, every one,
That we may rise from out the sea,
Gold-robed, for vast eternity.

On chariot clouds of gold we'll rise
  To that bright world above,
To meet the angels of the skies
  And sing redeeming love.

CHORUS.

My kingdom home, the angels' home,
My home high up in Heaven.

And as the myriads rise to sing
  In clouds of golden spray,
The kingdom bells shall sweetly ring
  Through Time's unfading day.

The Son of God shall be the light
   Of that bright world on high,
To fade the stars and banish night,
   And flood the golden sky.

There angels sweep through golden spray
   And glittering clouds of Heaven,
Where chariots roll through endless day
   And kingdom floats are driven.

Never Change the Flag.

[Presented to my brother, Mr. Joel H. Davis, and Charlotte his wife.]

Never change the flag—never, never;
It was shap'd to live forever;
Who could imagine, who could tell
The effect of its funeral knell?
Every sacred tie would be lost,
The nation would forget its cost,
Washington would be forsaken,
The foundation would be shaken.

That blood-stained banner of the wars
Which victory crown'd with thirteen stars,
Would fall as ruins o'er the grave,
Where din of war laid heroes brave,
With all the art that's left in man,
In this grand age of skillful hand,
No change of flag will ever do
For lovers of the starry blue.

Rivers of blood from fathers brave
Have covered the hills our flag to save;
Who, with our American pride,
Could change the flag for which they died?

No true American ever will
Forsake the flag of Bunker Hill,
Trenton, Yorktown and New Orleans,
Lafayette, Gates and General Green.

We'll never, never, never die
While the same flag waves 'neath the sky.
Webster, Jackson, and Henry Clay,
Adams, and all of ancient day,
Loved that bright flag which made them free,
And shed the light of liberty.
Your " Pansy," for a national flower
Cultured would live a lovely bower.

But all the pansies in creation
Could be no honor to the nation.
Our flag is worth ten thousand fold
Its length and breadth in sheets of gold.
But with a change, and honors lost,
Its wealth would drop from gold to dross.
With its fall all honors fall,
Strange flags would float o'er Federal Hall.

A conquered nation we should be
Minus the flag of liberty ;
High in the clouds the Goddess stands,
With light of freedom in her hands,
The flag of all the olden wars,
The same flag now with many stars
Still hangs before her faithful eye,
Fame towering to a cloudless sky.

No other flag, no other name
Could claim its battles and its fame.
So may it live as it begun,
To feed on stars one by one,
Until our Jupiter shall rise
To shine amid the national skies
From north to south, o'er land and sea,
To light the globe with liberty.

The Battle of Gettysburg.

[Presented to my brother-in-law, Mr. Zane Underwood, and my
sister Elizabeth, his wife.]

Out from the ports and rifle-pits,
　　Down from the rude-built mountain wall,
Down from the camp the Gray boys get,
　　While the stars look down and the moonbeams fall,
And on they sweep, like a cloud of war,
　　Tipping the skirts of the widespread plain;
A rumbling sound, with footstep jar,
　　As guides move on the death war-train.

Down the vale of the Mother State,
　　With armies ninety thousand strong,
And led by Lee, the skilled and great,
　　With martial tramp and drill and song.
Down they sweep, like a wall of steel,
　　With victory stamped on every face.
And army drill that knows no yield
　　When stamp'd in fiery Southern race.

On they sweep, o'er the rock-bed stream,
　　Through town and o'er the mountains tall,
With no foreboding in their dream
　　That this grand force should ever fall.

To Gettysburg they set their course,
  And when they reach'd that ill-fate town
They found MEADE's hundred thousand force
  Were moving on the highland ground.

LEE moved far up the sloping hill
  One hundred and fifty large guns,
To open fire when morn was still
  And night lit up by rising sun.
MEADE also watch'd for early morn,
  And planted guns on well-formed ground.
The cyclone rose, and thunder warned,
  And iron hail came pouring down,

Earth trembled 'neath the mighty jar,
  The atmosphere roll'd to and fro ;
The clouds were rent by din of war,
  The village rock'd beneath her foe.
Showering lead and muttering thunder,
  And hiding clouds of smoke arose,
Then LEE's full force came sweeping under,
  And closer drew the mighty foes.

MEADE's army stood like walls of fire,
  And from its flame death's thunder roll'd ;
The clouds of smoke rose thick and higher,
  While missl'd lead poured from the mould.
LEE's army moved, three columns deep,
  Beneath that withering flame of death,
The wiers bid the world to weep
  Ten thousand tears for every breath.

And lo! the mighty columns waved
  Four miles, and ninety thousand strong,
With all their skill and hearts so brave,
  Their sun had set, their day was gone.
Yet formed their lines and marched away
  With all their pride and Southern skill;
The starry Blue had crown'd the day,
  And MEADE was champion of the hill.

But as the mighty war-train swung
They tun'd their horns, and thus they sung:
"I wish I was in Dixie!   Away! away!
In Dixie's land we'll make our stand,
To live and die for Dixie's land!
Away, away! Away down South in Dixie!"

MEADE's army to the heaven's swung
One hundred flags, and thus they sung:
"Bright starry Blue, shield of the brave,
O'er freedom's land shall ever wave!
Let armies fall, by din of war,
But spare it not one single star!"

That blood-stained banner, symbol red,
Shall float o'er graves of fathers dead,
Who yet as slaves brought king to wars,
While heaven look'd down on thirteen stars.

It's led our nation safe through wars,
Still adding many brilliant stars,

The Union as it was begun,
We can't divide nor yet spare one.

O'er North and South it soon shall wave,
Home of the free, home of the brave;
Sons, Blue and Gray, shall close the war,
Flag minus not one single star.

And it was so; so may it stand
While freedom's banner shields the land;
Tears for the Blue, tears for the Gray,
Who gave their lives on that great day.

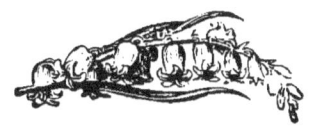

I am Dying.

[Lines written at the death of the poet's daughter, Lura, and embracing her dying words.]

I am dying, mother, dying;
  The repelling tide of life has passed;
Clouds of life, adrift and flying,
  Unveil the bright'ning sunset fast.

The gates beyond life's sunset swing,
I almost hear the angels sing;
I'm waiting now for them to come
And bear me to my Heavenly Home.

There shall I be as white as snow,
  And dread no more life's chilling blasts;
I'm waiting now, waiting to go;
  The angels' train is coming fast.

Hicks' Journal.

I read Hicks' Word and Works Journal,
   He dwells amid the planet stars,
But seeks the bright world eternal,
   Still far beyond the brilliant Mars.

So in the silent shades of dream
   My soul is wafted to the skies
To feast on grandeur of his theme,
   While round we sail and upward rise.

When lost from earth by tint of skies,
   To hang amid the starry blue,
On fairy wings to fairy eyes,
   The radiant worlds swift roll to view.

Transparent sweeps the comet trains,
   The motive power a globe of fire;
Trackless they sweep thro' Heaven's domain,
   Dividing space and drifting higher.

They glide from cities of the sky;
   The passengers have golden wings,
Their train around the planets fly,
   The star-bells of the heavens ring.

The blending tone of all the stars
   Bids them God's speed from bell to bell;
From Jupiter they sweep by Mars
   To bright ring'd Saturn, where they dwell.

The Old Stone Chimney.

We glanced around its wood-charred wall,
 Moss-grown, time-worn, and crumbling down;
With hearthstone deep and fire-cracks small,
 And fragments gray all scattered 'round.
The pick of time marked the jam-stone
 Year seventeen hundred and ninety-two,
When forest wilds were fully grown,
 And woodsmen numbered very few.

Silent and ghostly stands the wall,
 Death's wing had snapp'd life's tender thread;
Crumbling ruins. Ah, that was all
 To tell the story of the dead.
The jam that formed the cricket's cell,
 The lug-pole where the trammel swung,
The moss-grown walls that formed the well,
 In sad deserted fragments hung.

A soldier and wife—that was all—
 Both strangers in a forest land;
No kindred friend list to their call,
 No kindsman grasped the dying hand.
Beneath a walnut tree, well grown,
 Moss-gray and rustic, 'neath its shade
In solemn token stands a stone,
 And there the soldier's dust was laid.

Rude and time-worn it stands alone ;
 Green sods spread o'er the hero's grave ;
No sculptor's chisel marks the stone
 That stands in honor of the brave.
From Revolutionary wars
 This hero through the forest came ;
Came when the flag of thirteen stars
 Had scarcely won a national name.

While now he sleeps beneath the sod
 His flag o'er sixty millions wave ;
And sixty millions thank their God
 For heroes in the silent grave.
Then shall his dust sleep there unknown
 While his fame on national clouds should ride ?
Should not a monumental stone
 There represent the nation's pride ?

[Written for the Four Hundredth Anniversary of the Discovery of America by Columbus, October 21, 1892.]

A hero bold,
From lands of old,
Far away from his native land,
O'er the ocean green,
Which man had not seen,
Stood firm with an unwavering hand.

Last hope of land
Forsook his band,
And a rebellion seem'd to rise;
But he urged them on
To the coming dawn—
To the sun-blending land and skies,

Then a land breeze
Come o'er the seas,
And the sun from out the forest crept;
At tip of morn
A new world was born,
And his crew fell at his feet and wept.

A light soft breeze
From out the trees
Had kissed the face of the flowers,

And bore rich perfume
To a sea-sick home
As new life in a dying hour.

Then outline dim
On the western rim,
Blending land with the silvery skies,
More distinctly grew,
And the joyous crew
Tearfully gazed with longing eyes.

Columbus stood,
Profound in mood,
As he gazed on his promised land;
Then, with flag unfurled,
Placed it on a world
Ocean-hid from civilized man.

Columbus found
The globe was round,
One-half hing'd on his forest shore;
As the new dawn broke
The learned sage 'woke,
And bewildering clouds fell no more.

My eyes to-day
Swim far away
To that primeval forest shore
Where his boat touch'd land,
And the Red Man's hand
Show'd friendship at the wigwam door.

Where clustering trees
Spread to the seas,
North, south, east, west, valleys and plains,
And rivers unstained
Through the forest train'd,
Silvery and clear as the rains.

Four hundred years—
Strange it appears—
Sixty-five million souls to-day,
Sixty-five millions ;
Wealth, sixty-five billions,
And king of nations in display !

War in the South.

The cloud of slavery ending in storm,
  Like cyclone sweeping from shore to shore,
Came rushing void of justice or form,
  With earthquake shock and the battle's roar.

The bright, waving field of golden grain
  By murderous soldiery were trodden down,
Temples of justice in ashes lain,
  And flames rose from the ill-fated town.

The sharp scythe of war had mown its swarth,
  Wealth of slavery a thing of the past ;
The once solid wealth now seem'd but froth,
  And destruction's card seem'd to be cast.

But the fog of war soon cleared away,
  And the South rose with her pride and skill,
As seen to-day with a grand display
  Of its schools and towns, factories and mills.

Proudly may her ambition now rise,
  To equal the North, the East, or the West,
And glory in her bright, sunny skies—
  Land of the flowers, land of the blest.

𝔚hat is 𝔯eligion?

Religion is the sunshine of Heaven;
It illuminates the dark side of the soul,
It melts the drifting ice of sin and folly,
And sheds true light through bewildered eyes;
It is the golden key
That unlocks the pearly gate
Of the Heavenly Kingdom;
It is the robe of righteousness,
The golden wings of angels,
And a title to a crown in Heaven.

Mars in 1892.

On sweeps the scintillating stars;
Adown descends the brilliant Mars,
Sweeps nearer earth in radiant style,
One hundred and six million miles;

Yet thirty five million miles away,
Will charm the eye with grand display,
Reposing in refulgent beams,
Out rivaling all descriptive dreams.

This distant visitor appears,
As tempted, once in fifteen years,
To visit earth through southern skies,
To feast the scientific eyes.

A thousand telescopic eyes
Will pierce the deep ethereal skies
To fathom her in golden robe,
While visiting this mighty globe.

Night.

Night is the ghost of the world;
It boldly walks around the globe;
Flees from the eyes of the sun;
But at times it lifts its ghostly shades
To dim the brightness of the moon,
And walks amid the stars.

Day.

Day is the life of the world;
Commanded by the king of planets,
It puts the stars to flight;
It fades the brightness of the moon
And seals the planets in the skies;
The tear-like dewdrops of the night
Vanish from the face of the flowers,
And, as they unfold in grandeur,
Like the envious queen of a nation,
Would they gladly rob
The great king of the day
Of all his brightness and glory?
Coquettish, they kiss the bright sunbeams
And paint their cheeks with its gold.

A Messenger of Death.

He rode a gaily snow-white steed;
    Sister clung to my arm and said:
"Oh! who is that with such great speed?"
    When, quick as flash, they both had fled;

The sun was bright, 'twas then at noon;
    We stood beside our cottage door;
The flash was clear, but ah! too soon
    For our dull eyes the scene was o'er;

By roadside stood a building small;
    We saw them on the other side;
One bound from his great steed, so tall,
    Would span the distance in his ride.

We thought the great white steed had fell;
    One rod brought us within full view;
The road was clear, and then the spell
    Gave vent to all that fright could do.

Trembling and speechless we there stood,
    My sister clinging to my arm,
When far away a horseman rode
    As one who rode to give alarm.

Soon rounding to our old loved home,
    With trembling voice the rider said:
"With sad, sad news to-day I come;
    Your friend Alexander is dead."

Love.

Love hides itself within the heart;
　Unconsciously the eye reveals;
And like the shaft with missil'd dart,
　Cupid within the prison steals.

He fears no law; he has no key;
　He snaps the hinges from the door;
The prison set the inmate free,
　Confirms what she believed before.

The smothered flame bursts from its cell,
　Uniting with flame in return;
What both believed they now know well;
　Fuel to flame, so it must burn.

Loud word from the watch tower fall;
　The fire-bell gives the alarm;
The eye speaks louder yet than all,
　And rivets its words with a charm.

Life and Love.

What is life? Oh! what is life?
It is only a little blaze, dimly burning,
And liable to be blown out
In a moment at any time.
What is love? Oh! what is love?
It is that foretaste of Heaven
Which lives within the soul of man
As the golden link in the chain
Of relationship and wedlock
And without which human beings
Could only live to hate each other,
Despise God and all of His creation.
Love is the golden thread
Which winds on the celestial spool
In the heavenly kingdom,
Ever winding and ever drawing
The converted soul
Nearer to God and its final rest.
While the gall of nature,
By the blinding influence of Satan,
Rebels and pulls away ;
The thread of love is snapped,
And the soul may be forever lost.
The blaze of love becomes full

To feed the bitterness of hatred—
Not only to hate self,
But to hate God and Heaven
And all of God's creation;
And as the bright star of hope
Sinks beneath the golden
Clouds of the heavenly skies,
Darkness and gloom overshadows,
And love may be forever done—
And that is hell enough.
The golden thread of love
Is the telephone by which
God's power is communicated
To the never-dying soul;
Daily its vibrations are felt,
And the soul feeds on bread eternal,
And drinks the wine of heavenly bliss;
Lifting the soul above
The dark clouds of sorrow,
Even to catch a glimpse
Of the sunlight of Heaven.
The sun that shines
To set and shine again
Only lights a life of pain;
The sun that shines to ever shine
Lights a world and life divine—
God's love is the light,
Heaven glitters with its brightness,
And the bright angels drink
Of its fountain eternal.

[Written the Four Hundredth Anniversary of the Discovery of America by Columbus, October 21, 1892.]

The American eye
Should look from a happy face
As the dark shades
Of the past ages sweep before it.
Reverse the beam of time;
Go back four hundred years;
Take one glimpse
Of this vast continent
As Columbus found it
With the shy Red man,
Who, with noiseless step,
Down to the seashore crept,
While a blood-chilling yell
'Mid the dense forest fell
From a wild and savage race;
But the smiling face
Of the unknown race,
And their wondrous ship
From the unknown world,
With its mighty wings
Flapping the winds of the ocean,
Bore with it a charm,
And the strangers were welcomed to land.

The densely-drooping forest,
Now swept from sea to sea,
With the Fall carpet spread
As the hand of nature wove it
Of gold and crimson leaves,
With the silvery brooks
Creeping through a forest of gold;
And the wild woodland flowers,
Kiss'd by the frost of Autumn,
Fading and dropping
Their beauty and rich perfume;
The sweet and charming song
Of the richly-plumed forest birds;
And the high-towering eagle king,
With his throne high on the hoary ledge,
Call'd forth admiration
And love of the forest.
The hideous scream of the panther,
The howl of daring wolf,
The dull tramp of the buffalo,
The surly growl of the bear,
And the grand herds of elk and deer
Charmed the eye and filled the heart
With love for a forest life.
Even with picture before us
We have only a faint glimpse
Of four hundred years ago.
But like mountain brooks
Sweeping forest leaves to the seas,

So the white man's ax
Has swept the forest trees;
And like a tornado of fire
In a drifting snowstorm,
The forests have melted
By the white man's torch;
So lands of the wigwam,
Once the home of the Red man,
To-day lift their glittering spires
To the clouds of the heavens;
While the rich fringe of wealth,
Like a kingly palace of old,
Adorns the cities with silver and gold;
Like a new created heaven
Happy homes are smiling
With Christian love and intelligence;
Railroads checker the land;
Churches and school-houses
Dot the plains and the valleys;
The wondrous tongue of wire
Speaks to loved ones far away;
The nation's mighty cable
Holds communion with our mother
Across the briny deep;
The Pacific and Atlantic
Shake hands by rail;
The towering gods and snow-capped peaks
Of the Rocky Mountains
Look east and west, north and south,

O'er waving fields of grain,
Railroads, towns, and cities,
While the white man's pick,
With untiring stroke,
Seek silver and gold
At their treasured feet.
While the Red man of the forest,
Still wrapped in his heathen robe,
Tattered in furs and buckskin fringe,
Sullenly hunkers around
His dull and smoky wigwam fire;
Wrapped in his buffalo robe
On his scanty mat of furs,
He slumbers and groans
Only to dream of the sad
History of his fallen race;
At the hour of the awakening sun
He rises to behold
The wondrous tide of the white man,
Like a storm-driven cloud,
Sweeping o'er his nearest plain;
He foams and drifts before it;
He pursues his westward flight
Only to behold
The glittering snow-capped peaks
And the towering gods
Of the brook-worn gorge
Majestically rising before him;
In his maniac rage

He again turns to the plains,
But the tide of the white man sweeps on,
Which he numbers
By the sands of the sea;
His last buffalo has been slain
By the death-pealing thunders
Of the white man's gun;
With anger painted in his eye,
And a bronze-like surly face,
He mounts the iron horse;
He sweeps through the plains of the West
And the charming hills of the East
Only to curse the day of our glory,
While the Goddess of Liberty
Lifts her mighty arm
To the clouds of the heavens
With everlasting flame
Streaming from her finger tips,
Emblematic of freedom,
As a light to the world,
And which proclaims
In tones of thunder
That Columbus land
Shall ever be
A home for the Red man
And a home for the free.

A Gate in the Clouds.

[Dedicated to Rev. W. L. Burdick, Ph. B., D. B.]

The parting day pass'd through liquid gold
  As the soft twilight grew rosy and bright,
When a scene too grand for earth to hold
  Trail'd slowly before the coming night.

Cloud-built walls, like gods of the mountains,
  With silvery cliffs and golden edge,
Rose in the sky as though a fountain
  On every side supported a ledge.

A gate 'mid the walls now gently swings,
  While shimmering rays, like burnished gold,
Shoots forth and tipping a thousand wings
  Of the fleecy trains as up they roll.

A misty fringe o'er the gateway hung,
  Radiantly tipped and of grand display,
As through a gate in its beauty swung
  As the passway for the parting day.

Dark wings of night o'erspread the sky;
  A solemn stillness filled the land
As though day lived only to die
  And cling to the gate with a parting hand.

Dear Lady.

Dear lady, power to thee was given,
And by that power we are driven
To love thee much, or as thou will,
But one who loves must love thee still.

That magic power of thine alone
To thee, perhaps, may be unknown;
But thou hast the key and the chain,
The seal once stamp'd must e'er remain.

Could'st thou but know thy magic power,
As charms impress in fatal hour,
Thou would'st at least a sinner be
To scorn the sympathy for thee.

Proof that there is a God.

The sun ablaze forever burns,
The globe rolls 'round it and returns,
The moon sweeps 'round this earthly ball
To prove that God is Lord of all.

The chandeliering stars, ten million strong,
Too deep in space to paint in song,
Gleam brightly and forever shine
To prove the wondrous hand divine.

The Fox.

As the fox devoureth
So shall he be devoured.

A red-leaf bush bent o'er the ledge
  On which two pheasants went to roost;
The ice was deep, and near its edge
  A fox came hunting for a goose;
He saw the pheasants in the bush,
  When down he sat upon the ice;
"Come down," said he, "and what you wish
  From out my basket shall be nice."

"No," said the birds up in the tree,
  "We fear that you are hungry too,
And while we feast on grapes from thee
  We shall no longer number two."
"No," said the fox, "I will be true,
  And all my supper shall be nice,
And you shall also number two
  When you shall wish to leave the ice."

"To prove me true come down just one,
  I swear you shall take no alarm;
My meal is ready and well done,
  Those whom I love I could not harm."

Then cuts were drawn up in the tree,
    For doubts they had of fox's thirst,
And neither one just then felt free,
    To test the stranger's honor first.

Then swiftly came the proud king bird;
    This meal was blessed with grapes and wine;
The fox then smiled but never stirred,
    But pass'd the grape long from the vine.
The bird's fear fled, when in a glee
    He nestled to the fox's side;
And glancing upward in the tree
    He fearless showed his kingly pride.

And then he fell into a doze;
    The fox had never changed his seat;
The ice had melted and then froze;
    The bird he pick'd and quickly eat.
Now, says the fox, "for this my sin
    I must tear loose and then away,
The morning light will soon begin,
    And then will come the glare of day.

"I know the hounds are far away;
    The wolf and cur I do not fear;
But test my sins by light of day
    Is more than I can ever bear."
The deed is done, the fox is fast,
    The rosy sun looks o'er the hills,
The woodsman sweeps down like a blast
    And with his club the fox he kills.

So by the fox of this fast age
  Proudest sons are misled for gain,
Shackled as slaves on freedom's stage,
  Powerless to sever the chain.
The hungry fox still leads him on,
  Secreting his ill-gotten gain,
And fearing truth when day shall dawn,
  That temples of justice shall reign.

Mirrored Shadows of Heaven.

As I stood upon a mountain peak
I beheld a grandly-painted cloud
Moving from the golden sunset;
And as the dying embers of the day
Cast a lingering ray
As though loth to exchange
Its golden hue for the dark
Silken shades of the night,
The moon and stars half lit up
Grew dim and went out.
With brightness to dazzle the sun,
The bright golden cloud moved on;
The green fringy hills
And the low-trailing valleys
Become variegated and bloomed
With its bright golden hues;
The face of the earth was kissed
By the lips of its grandeur;
And as its arms of beauty
Embraced the gods of nature,
The towering peaks stood
Like crown'd kings envious of grandeur
That they could not possess nor control;
Yet stealing its golden edge
And smiling at the glory
That painted their crimson ledge.

Faith.*

[Presented to my daughter Minnie, who copied the manuscript for this book.]

We stood upon the mountain ledge
   Of moss-grown walls that tower'd high;
She placed her foot upon the edge
   And glanced with confidential eye.

" Please hold my hand," she softly said,
   Then o'er the towering wall she hung,
No seeming fear nor slightest dread,
   As to my slender arm she swung.

Then, as her life hung on my arm,
   I whispered gently to her ear,
" Should 1 let go, oh! what alarm
   Would chill your home and mother dear."

A glance from her bright loving eyes
   Told more than words can ever tell;
She shrunk not back, but glanc'd the skies
   With voice clear as a silver bell.

---

* The subject of this sketch was the charming Miss Josie Randolph, of Plainfield, N. J. We stood upon the brink of the towering cliff one hundred feet high.

She looked again down o'er the wall
  Then in her gentle tone she said,
"I'm sure you will not let me fall,
  And so, dear sir, I have no dread."

I stood upon the ledge of hell,
  With sinful eyes looked o'er the wall;
I saw the pit where Devils dwell,
  And shuddered least I there should fall.

I prayed to Christ: "Hold thou my hand,
  O Saviour; do not let me fall;
Thine is the power, as now I stand,
  To stay my life, my soul, my all."

The wings of Heaven, with golden light,
  Sun-tipped my soul with love and joy,
And changing scenes of visions bright
  Swept heavenly bliss without alloy.

Golden spray from the heavens fell,
  Mingled with love and joy divine;
Vibrant chords from the kingdom bell
  Divinely whispered, "Thou art mine."

My life hangs by a slender thread,
  I look down o'er a slippery wall,
I have no fear, I have no dread,
  My Saviour will not let me fall.

Little Tracks in the River Sand.

'Twas in the dark days of bloodshed and gloom,
 When the night-owl mocked the war-whoop and yell,
And flames at the stake but pictured the doom
 Of a blood stained race in the pits of hell.
Horrors too deep for the name of crime,
 And sorrows too deep for the wailing tear;
But sweeping wrath on the wings of time,
 With that revenge in store that conquers fear.

Oft they came, prowling like wolves at night,
 Wrapped in furs, wolf-hide robes, and buffalo horn,
War-paint face, red-eyed demons of fright,
 Stealing a march at early flash of morn,
Chief a horned beast in form of man,
 With imps of the devil trailing his heels,
Sweeping life like the drifting sands
 Are blown from the plains and the sun-dried fields.

But wrath o'erruled, and the tide swept on
 Adown, down the beautiful woodland vale,
Where glimpes of the sun at early dawn
 Crept through the forest like a dingy trail.
There the white man's axe, with muffled sound,
 Awoke the wild herds on the forest hill;
And the wolf and panther sneaked around
 In the dead of night with a vicious will.

But they reared their camp in the forest deep,
    And near by the wall their sentinel stood ;
He knew no night, he knew no sleep,
    But stood as the shades of the forest wood.
And he knew the smell that spoke of harm,
    And no deaf ear to tramp or a sound.
By a signal note he raised alarm,
    Which the sleepers read from their camping-ground.

Awake, but still as the camp-fire blaze,
    Till the red-eyed beasts lit their eyes by the flame.
As they stood in the dark with a gaze
    Half charmed, half bewildered, amazed, and tamed.
Then a sweeping blaze, and a deathly roar ;
    Then all was still, the flashing eyes gone out,
And the panther's gaze was seen no more
    As he fled from the gun and deathly scout.

Then cabins were built from forest trees,
    And the gray walls lined with emerald moss ;
And they had no foolish pride to please,
    For the hearts of all were minus dross.
Then the old cock blew his daybreak horn,
    And he clapped his wings for the fading night,
And the woodsman rose with the early morn
    With a happy face and prospects bright.

And all content in their rural home,
    With the centre star a lovely mother.
And they had no foolish hearts to roam,
    Yet love untold loved they one another.

Sweet, rosy girls, with bright golden hair;
  Children bright-eyed, loved, and fondly embraced;
Young mothers loving, and angel fair;
  And fathers true, of a brave, sturdy race.

Peace prevailed in their rude forest home,
  As music rose from the rumbling river;
And birds of the trees the forest roamed
  In golden plume and gloss-dress feather.
But, alas! the great alarm bell swung
  And the bravest hearts felt a deathly chill,
And little ones to their mothers clung,
  As signals rose from a distant hill.

Hark! hark! they come like red fiends of hell,
  Prowling around the rustic cabin door,
With hideous voice and chilling yell
  As wrath from the bloody demons roar.
With battering ram burst puncheon door,
  Slay the strong, bind the weak with twigs and thongs,
While their garments wipe blood from the floor
  And their sobs are mocked by a hissing song,

Then to the stake others, bound with chain,
  Stand with streaming eyes, gaze upon the dead,
While torch flames shoot streaks of pain
  And burnt eyes burst from a living head.
Then away, away through the forest deep,
  With the lovely maid with bright golden hair,
And little children too sad to weep
  While hurried away from a home so dear.

The happy homes were left scenes of blood,
  Mangled corpse and black, charred bones at the stake.
Then the wrath of men rose like a flood,
  As they hurried on trail to overtake.
Through a primeval forest, unknown,
  They hurried o'er hill and through the dark vale,
Camp-grounds were found but the demons gone,
  And nothing left but the red devil's trail.

And lo! they reached a mighty river
  With golden sands and glittering pebble shore,
The two great forest lands to sever,
  While its swift and bold rushing waters pour.
But the fiends of death had crossed the flood,
  With boys and girls, torn from their native land,
And all that was left was stains of blood
  And the little tracks in the river sand.

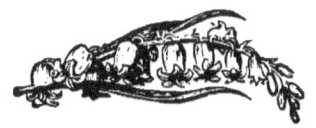

The Angels.

[Presented to Mrs. W. L. Burdick.]

Tune: "The Chariot."

We are sailing life's sea;
　　Soon we'll reach Heaven's shore,
Where the angels shall be,
　　And the God they adore,
And the bright clouds of gold
　　Bear the wings of the soul.

Chorus.—The angels on golden wings
　　　　Shall sweep through the clouds.

There the chariots shall roll
　　With the brightness of fire,
And the glorified soul
　　Pierce the clouds drifting higher,
Till the love-mingled skies
　　Feast the bright angel eyes.

Chorus.—The angels on golden wings
　　　　Shall sweep through the clouds.

Bright'ning through golden spray
　　Sweeps the myriads divine,
Symbols of that bright day
　　Which eternally shine;
And the shrill harp and song
　　Charm the heavenly throng.

Chorus.—The angels on golden wings
　　　　Shall sweep through the clouds.

The Lost Damsel,

A damsel, eighteen summers old,
   O'er highland wilds and valleys roam'd,
Her sparkling eyes of beauties mould
   Were lost to course and distant home.
The forest wings spread o'er her deep;
When hope was lost she stop'd to weep.

As tear-drops stole from loving eyes
   A voice unheard yet seemed to speak,
"On that tall peak that props the skies
   Thy lover there for thee doth seek."
She reached the heights with longing eyes,
As soft winds bore her weary cries.

A young man who had loved her dear
   Drew near, and now he heard her cry;
He clasped her hand and wip'd the tear,
   While joy was sparkling in her eye.
The love within the young man's soul
Grew stronger at least tenfold.

With sobs she said to him, "I'm lost;
   The sun sinks radiant in the sky;
I climb'd this peak to count the cost,
   Make one more effort e'er I die;
I've roam'd the forest all the day,
My life should soon have ebb'd away."

7

"Oh, no," said he, "you shall not die,
  Nor seek the peaks as the lost dove;
I'll see you home, and then may I
  Hope for a token of your love?"
She sweetly bow'd with loving eyes,
No words were needed for the wise.

He kissed the rosebloom of her lips;
  Hearts variegated like the flower;
The pink of love each other sips,
  Wedding its bloom with lasting power;
So drossless tints of cupid shade
On blooming love were thus inlaid.

Now, this was forty years ago,
  And still they walk the sands of life,
Though silvery locks o'er bright eyes flow,
  The damsel lost, a loving wife,
Love they plighted on the mountain
Still o'erflows their golden fountain.

Sails for Life.

When you set your sails for life
　　Look not for sunshine altogether,
For in this world or rush and strife
　　We must have clouds and stormy weather,

Believe not fairy tales of luck,
　　But rather trust honest labor;
Battles are gained by men of pluck,
　　And skillful use of the sabre.

Look not for large nuggets of gold,
　　Nor wealth that blooms in a day;
Pick up small grains that you can hold;
　　Reach not for things too far away.

Seek not for golden streaks of luck;
　　Far better seek a balance wheel
And gear it with the cogs of pluck,
　　And slip no skeins from off the reel.

Turn, turn the reel, and it will gain
　　Drawing threads from the spinning wheel;
No time is lost by tangled skein
　　While threads are left upon the reel.

Wind your thread in a solid ball,
　　Turn the ball with the balance wheel,
Shed no tears because your ball seems small,
　　Just keep on winding from the reel.

Not One! Not One!

Not one! not one! oh! who will dwell
Upon the land and on the sea
One hundred years to come?
Not one! not one now living!
Oh! who will rule the nation then,
The temples of justice to adorn?
Will freedom's sons bow to a king?
The bells of freedom fear to ring?
Will this republic build a throne
And freedom's honors all disown,
One hundred years to come?
Will Anarchy step up to rule,
Or Communism her temples build,
And raise the whirling clouds of hell,
Laden with cyclones to sweep
The Stars and Stripes from freedom's land?
No, never! never!
The infernal bloom of Communism
Will bear its poisonous fruit
To be cast into the wine-press
Of satan and his followers.
Though all now living will be in their graves,
Yet the Stars and Stripes will forever wave.

The Night of Life.

We journey through the night of life,
Weighing sorrow in the light side
Of the balance, joyous with the
Bright hope of that morning
Which brings eternal day.
If this life was all happiness
We would have no thirst
For the joys of eternity.
If this world was all brightness
Heaven would be robbed of its glory.
We feed on the crumbs of Heaven
Only as a foretaste of the joys
And grandeur which overflow the
Golden shores of the river of life.

From the Cradle to the Grave.

The cradle rocks a little girl;
   She leaves the cradle for the school;
She meets a boy fair as an earl,
   So love their passions now must rule;
So, like the bloom within the bud,
They try to hide this little flood.

The Two Lovers.

Deep in the heart of a blooming pink,
   Where no eye could e'er discover,
There hung a little golden link
   Dangling in the son-beams of her lover;
Deep as the link the son-beams stole,
And in the end his heart was mold.

The Bloom of Love.

The bloom of love is ever strange;
   Its tender stem you cannot sever;
Its golden hue will never change;
   It may be lost, yet live forever;
It may be hidden in the tomb,
And yet, alas! will ever bloom.

MARRIAGE.

Two budding flowers, side by side,
  Though different name and different bloom,
But when love touched their inward pride
  They both were changed and they were one;
So when the blossom opened wide
The fairest bloom her name denied.

HONEYMOON.

They bloomed with love as two bright flowers,
  Wedding in bliss, becoming one,
Melting in each other's powers;
  With honeymoon bright as the sun,
On the mountain of love they stood,
In their valley of love a flood.

TEN YEARS AFTER MARRIAGE.

Though flames of love blaze not so high,
  Yet constant blaze has left a coal,
Ash-hidden, and it cannot die,
  For like a diamond set in gold,
Though one-half hidden, still ablaze,
As bright as stars to light the days.

SILVER WEDDING.

They launched their boat upon the stream,
  To journey through the fogs of life,
'Neath stars of love and mist agleam,

Hung a silver link bright and rife.
Their sky was now so bright and clear,
A honeymoon lit their silver year.

GOLDEN WEDDING.

Their wedded bliss marked fifty years,
    And their year now bronzed with gold;
Snowflakes follow on silver hair,
    As the cares of time onward roll'd;
And though life's sun began to sink,
Their hearts hung in a golden link.

BRINK OF THE GRAVE.

Machines time-worn, tottering, and slow,
    Brows furrowed deep with many cares,
Bright-colored hair now white as snow,
    The bloom of five and ninety years,
They stand upon the wondrous brink,
Where life and death hangs in one link.

Liberty Bell.

High o'er the city in her steeple,
  With liberty budding for the bloom,
Her tongue to speak for all the people,
  As heroes in their council doom.

The day was long and long ago;
  Soon must the bell now tell the story;
Breathless the surging crowd below
  Look'd to the bell for words of glory.

The bellman to the rope now stands;
  Streets sparkle with uplifted eyes;
When, lo! her voice rang o'er the lands,
  "Liberty! liberty!" she cries.

Her voice was drown'd in acclamation;
  Her sides were rent by heavy stroke;
The sons of slavery, now a nation,
  Resolved to die or rend the yoke.

She voiced a light, as though a flame
  Had burst from regions of the earth,
And with that fiery tongue proclaim'd
  Equal rights and our nation's birth.

And though she never rang again,
  She sent defiance to the king,
Snapp'd the yoke, severed the chain,
  And bid freedom's bells to ever ring.

Wealth.

Wealth is the gigantic arm
That wields the National sword.
A nation poverty-stricken
Would be too weak to stand alone,
And would become a slave
To kings and tyrany.
If all men were millionaires
Who would fill the cogwheels
That move the nations of the earth?
Wealth is the power,
Poor men the machinery;
While all work together
The world moves harmoniously;
Shut off, the power and machinery stops,
And the poor man must beg for bread.
The poor man who wields the sword
In opposition to wealth
Only lifts the weapon
To sever his own head.

Dream of the Eternal World.

I dreamed of the eternal world,
  Where all the angels soar on wing,
And golden clouds in breeze unfurl
  While myriads float above and sing.

My glimpse of earth could now behold
  All the dear friends I ever knew,
Few were left who in days of old
  I loved so dear, for they were true.

Most all of them had crossed the stream,
  Were robed in glory's brightest crown,
Which side, should I wake from the dream,
  In Heaven or still on earth be found.

My spirit clung to earth no more,
  Yet earthly friends entwined my heart;
Alas! my dream too soon was o'er,
  And earth still held my counterpart.

Washington's Birthday, February 22, 1732.

Our nation's pride was not a king
   Who sat upon a throne of gold,
But one of whom the poets sing,
   Whose fame and worth can ne'er be told.
He rose high like a star of light,
   Yet knew full well his country's call;
He pledged his life for what was right
   And sipped the cup of war for all.

He planned the flag of thirteen stars,
   And in defiance let her swing,
To face the storm of Britain wars,
   That came like cyclones swift of wing.
All hail that bright and glorious morn,
   The morn that for our freedom spoke,
The day that Washington was born,
   Born to sever the kingly yoke.

Now let our seventy millions rise,
   Raise tunes of thankfulness and sing
Until the echoes reach the skies,
   For one truly greater than a king.
Peace at home, good will to all,
   His motto and his life foretold,
Yet shrunk not from his country's call,
   But freed her from the king of old.

We worship not the man of earth,
 But worship God, and God alone,
Yet on the day of Washington's birth
 Great national honors should be shown.
To the oily wick of liberty
 He touched the everlasting flame,
And set a world of slavery free.
 Thus wrote with gold his page of flame.

Generations of the Dead.

[Dedicated to my brother-in-law, Rev. James B. Davis, and my
sister Emily, his wife.]

The sun winged away, through clouds of gold,
    The evening train rumbl'd far away,
When alone we strolled 'mid tombs of old,
    Where the fathers sleep of ancient day.
They knew no sound of the rumbling train,
    Nor the flash of the news-bearing wire.
Homes in the forest they sought to gain;
    The shy wild herds took fright at their fire.

King of the forest alone now stand
    Beneath his shade in each narrow cell;
The woodsman of a primeval land,
    To the reaper, 'neath his branches fell.
His forest bow'd to their sturdy stroke;
    By their torches melted to ashen bed,
Now lifts the spires of this giant oak
    As monuments o'er his sleeping dead.

Once he here stood as a forest king,
    Shaded and clustered on every side,
Interwoven with the bloom of spring,
    And green wall'd from every stormy tide,
Widely now his mighty arms are spreads,
    And deeply rooted amid the tombs.

His forest gone, but sleepers instead,
   And the marble stone replace his bloom.

We stood beneath his clustering shade,
   A dove in his leafy branches sung,
Mourn'd o'er the tomb where mother was laid
   In the long ago, when I was young.
Life's sun set on her fair angel brow
   Like sunbeams on a violet laid,
She paled, and then to the reaper bow'd,
   To sleep beneath this hallowed shade.

And near that lonely murmuring pine
   A furrowed brow, a silvery head,
Age-worn, and in the years of decline;
   Beneath that stone my father was laid.
Proudly he drove his turf-rolling plow,
   Herds of the field knew his feed-time voice,
Golden grain before his sickle bow'd;
   As the sun dipp'd low his home rejoiced.

Let pride despise not his well-paid toil,
   Nor we disown our grand native hills
Rich with green meadows, rich with the soil,
   Bright silvery brooks and rippling rills.
Where, oh! where are the silvery grays;
   A voice speaks from the mouldering tomb,
"Done with earth and have returned to clay
   With the millions, and yet there is room."

Bright jewels in the morning of life,
  As stars fade before the rising sun,
They battled not with the world of strife,
  But, oh! too soon life's bright race is run.
The clustering locks of golden hair
  Oft bloomed o'er forms too lovely to fade,
But drank they not of the cup of care,
  But, like lilies, dropp'd to valted shade.

Vaulted in the silent earthly deep
  Their bones speak to the haughty and proud;
We heed their voice, nature bids us weep,
  The warring thunders are rolling loud.
No monuments of honors regal,
  But hands which the gavel might have swayed
Grew weary, grew tremulous and pale,
  And their honors were sealed with the spade.

Here sleeps the sons of the olden wars,
  Fresh from the battle-fields of glory,
Who fought for the flag of thirteen stars
  As it waved o'er the fields all goary.
The din of war disturbs not their sleep,
  Ambitious battle forever done;
No rude lover for his lover weep,
  No rosy east warns them of the dawn.

One fair lady, with a half-bowed head,
  A wreath of flowers in her dimpled hand,

Hung o'er the tomb of her mother dead,
  Seal'd from her gaze by sods of the land.
The day was fading through golden skies;
  Weeping she stood o'er her mother dear;
To the golden clouds, with angel eyes,
  She looked through space to see her there.

Tears more affecting were never shed,
  For dead untombed we have learned to weep,
But the silent grave cares for our dead;
  In neglected vaults long do they sleep.
Rouse, ye sons, from thy dead slumber rise,
  And sleep ye not this side of the tomb;
Care for thy loved dead, who for the skies
  Bid earth adieu for a brighter home.

Weep not for them, but weep for their grave;
  Some neglected spot may mark their tomb;
Treat not thy sire as thou would'st a slave,
  And to thy son look for the same doom.
Though they are dead, bid them live again;
  Lift their fallen monumental stones;
Forsake not thy dead for earthly gain,
  Nor thy father and mother disown.

That gay church spire, with its rustic bell,
  Long since its century notes have sung,
And for the tomb, with a tolling knell
  O'er deep wailing sorrow, has it swung.

8

Clouds of sorrow have dim'd the church hall,
 Tears have rained, but clouds pass not away;
Dim have they grown, but they cannot fall
 This side the gates of the judgment day.

Should sleepers rise from their lowly bed
 When the voice of the bell wings thro' the air,
And the congregation of the dead
 Assemble in the old church-yard for prayer,
Far outnumbered would the living be—
 Generations now would know them not,
And a voice would come to you and me,
 "How soon, oh! how soon are the dead forgot!"

Pike's Peak.

[Dedicated to my only son, B. H. Davis.]

Oh hoary peak! Thou king of kings,
Standest thou in thy matchless form,
Commanding the snow-capped peaks around thee,
Dazzling the eyes of men,
And baffling the skillful pen
Thy wonderous grandeur to describe.
Bathing thy feet in the rippling brook,
And chanting weird songs on the silvery tongue
Of thy snow-fed streams and misty falls.
The cyclone howls around thy form,
Dipping their smutty wings
Far beneath the crowning peak
Of thy time-worn massive walls.
The lightnings flash and the thunder rolls,
And the clouds drift on in silky scrolls,
And the raindrops dance on the silvery stone,
While the king looks down from his sunlit throne.
Eyes of the prehistoric cave dwellers
Gazed upon thy wonderous altitude
With adoration at the close of the day.
Then lift thy crown to the skies,

And catch the last glimmering rays
Of the golden sunbeams;
And wrap thy golden mantle around thee,
Then drop thy golden robe,
And turn thy face and kiss the moon,
And wrap thyself in nightly vales
Of ghostly shades and silvery gleamings.
The sun sweeps o'er the dark blue sea
And burns the misty shades of night.
And pours a flood of golden light
Upon thy misty, sparkling crown;
While the towering gods of the brook-worn gorge,
And the sweeping fields of the distant plains,
In their dewy robes peacefully slumber,
Still wrapped in the misty shades of the fading night.

The Closing Scene.

[Dedicated to my daughter Lura.]

The rolling hills were robed in gold,
  And fringed with curtains gold and green,
And highland peaks stood grand and bold,
  With crimson valleys trailed between;
Those golden robes hung from the sky
  Like drapery from a kingly throne;
Which charmed the lover's faithful eye,
  And, spell-bound, held him to his own.

Surrounding peaks propped all the sky,
  Both north and south, and east and west;
And Heaven's dome, hung from on high,
  On golden pillars seemed to rest.
The hills built up in fleecy trains,
  And waved in beauty, step by step,
And brightening by the cooling rains,
  The dazzling sunshine o'er them crept.

The sun went down o'er reefs of gold,
  And early in the new bright morn
His eyes seemed proud still to behold
  A world with scenes so bright adorned;

But Jack with snowy sickle came
   And reap'd his harvest gold and brown,
And wove a carpet of the same
   And spread it o'er the highland ground.

Then all the forest, grey and bare,
   Stood like dim ghosts scratching the sky,
And forest birds, so sweet and fair,
   Began to plume and southward fly;
Red-wing blackbirds, ten thousand strong,
   Had mustered for a long farewell;
In musical glee their farewell song
   Out on the breeze began to swell.

Such music, though, is not for me
   Ever to picture with a pen;
Their song was shrill, chords sweet and free,
   And charmed the stony hearts of men.
The birds were gone, Jack came again,
   And wove a carpet, grey and brown,
And scattered frost-thorns on the pane,
   And cut the bloming dahlia down.

The farmer hewed his winter log
   And drove his herd from field to barn;
The boys skipped out with rabbit dog,
   Kind mothers knit warm socks of yarn;
Sweet maidens all, with sparkling eyes,
   Stepped lightly o'er the kitchen floor,

And baked the bread and nice mince pies,
   And placed the fuel by the door.

Next night King Jack returned again
   And wove a carpet glossy white,
Without a spot, without a stain,
   And glistened in the darkest night.
The woodsman to the forest hill,
   With gun and bowie and dog beside;
The farmer jingling to the mill;
   The boys hunt crooked boards to ride.

The lover, with his nice brown steed
   Hooked to the cutter, flies away
To meet the one he loves indeed
   And take her riding in the sleigh.
The day is closed; day's work is done;
   The farmer from the grinding mill;
The lovers back, and they are one;
   The woodsman's deer hangs on the hill.

The Silent Messenger.

There is a magnet charm,
Or affinity, not form,
    That underlies
    The piercing eyes
That speaks the lasting word,
Yet never, never heard.

'Tis not the eye alone
That makes our wishes known,
    But something deep
    That seems to sleep
Within the mortal soul,
Unseen, yet all is told.

'Tis not the midnight dream,
Nor polished words, that seem
    To form this line
    Of heart and mind,
But something ever still,
And yet we know its will.

Speak No Ill.

Nay, speak no ill of friend or foe,
  And if you're driven to the wall,
  And there can find no good at all
Unstained by tongue, best let him go.

A kindly word is much preferred
  By those who seem to be in fault;
  And if at fault, may call a halt
And straighten every crooked word.

The slanderous tongue like bells are rung.
  Where all the town and country round
  Can hear the slang echo rebound
To sever hearts where friendship clung.

The tattler's tales are like the sails
  Of pirate ships upon the seas,
  They always sail on evil breeze,
Disguised by satanic veils.

When fortune turns and trouble burns
  The wreaking, pained, and withering heart,
  How soon does friendship then depart?
To count his faults his virtues spurn.

Can we disown the seed we've sown
  When harvest comes and fields are brown?
  Is there one perfect to be found?
Let him alone cast the first stone.

Terrors of a Criminal on Awakening from a Dream.

Great God! is this my awful doom?
  Yes, doomed to this dark, dismal cell,
To dream of joy and peace at home,
  While haunted by the ghosts of hell!

Tormented by the blood I drew;
  Tormented by that awful crime;
Tormented by the maid I slew,
  Who prayed me for an inch of time.

She told me that her heart was true;
  That she could love no other man—
Oh! cursed be the knife that drew
  Her precious blood upon my hand!

For still I see that pleading look,
  As if her tender heart would break;
She kissed me; then my hand she took,
  And threw her arm around my neck.

"Away!" I cried; "deceiver, stand!
  I know of thy dishonest heart.
Your love is for another man,
  So death shall sever us apart."

She sank beneath my wicked frown,
　Still glancing at the fearful knife,
And cried for mercy, sinking down,
　To close the scenes of mortal life.

But now the dreadful deed is done,
　A jealous heart must bear the blame;
For she was true, she loved but one,
　And he's now doomed to death and shame.

Oh, yes; in dreams I see my bed,
　Mid all the flaming fiends of hell.
They're in my cell! I see the dead!
　And soon must I their numbers swell!

War Eagle.

Now all the Nation, North and South,
  Had trimmed their lamps for civil war;
And death belched from the cannon's mouth,
  'Till heaven and earth quailed in despair.
Then came the mystic eagle spy,
  And joined a regiment of blue,
To climb the stairway of the sky,
  And lead the battles of the true.

And now the battle had begun;
  The eagle took the winding stair,
And sailed beyond the Southern gun,
  Around and round, high in the air.
Ten thousand Southern bullets flew
  To kill the golden eagle spy;
But still he led his army through,
  On wings where bullets could not fly.

And when the stars and stripes had won,
  And armies went encamped by night,
They found the eagle on his gun,
  Hung in the tent for roost at night.
He led each battle in its turn,
  Through all the din and clash of war,

His regiment's pet, he soon had learned
    The men and stripes which bore the star.

And when the cruel war was done,
    This bird went home with boys in blue,
Who crowned him king of victories won
    For starry blue and armies true.
And to the great centennial Fair
    They took this wondrous kingly spy,
Who made his throne high in the air.
    Above the din and battle cry.

Johnstown Flood, 1888.

They hurried to the garret ceiling,
  Six children and a lovely mother,
But soon the deathly waves there stealing,
  Filled space, 'till all began to smother,
And their doom was sealed; no ray of light,
  But a foaming flood was passing by,
And darkness of that fearful night
  Had cast its shades o'er moon and sky.

They bent their way to the window pane,
  And the mother seized a floating board,
And one of the band admission gained;
  A kiss, good-bye, and was heard no more.
Six times, as the floating timbers passed,
  She placed them on, and a kiss, good-bye;
But worst of all was the dear one last—
  A father's pet with mischievous eye.

Just then a crash and the building fell,
  And was swept away 'mid clash of sound;
But she clung to the roof, which floated well,
  And swift away from the floating town,
Out on the waves in the pitch of night,
  'Mid shrieks and screams and dying groans,

And not a lamp, nor a glimmering light,
   As buildings groaned with a hideous moan.

But away on the wings of the waves,
   With the star of Hope forever set,
And just a span to the hissing grave,
   Where wrath of the waves its victim met,
Down, down the wrathy current flying,
   Grinding, surging, hissing and roaring,
Screaming, groaning, moaning and dying,
   The angry waves 'mid forests pouring.

On the distant shore a signal light,
   But the forest trees walked through the flood
With clutching fingers and arms of might
   Wrecking the crafts and the floating wood.
A voice was heard on the wave-washed shore.
   And a signal light was gleaming bright,
And her craft rushed mid din and roar;
   But was saved by men in pitch of night.

When We Were Boys.

When we were boys, one dreary night,
We made a pine torch for a light,
And ventured up the silent stream,
Which bent its course through evergreen.
Our fishing party, brave as men,
Bore torches and a gig in hand.
An awful stillness now prevailed,
The brook lay slumbering in the vale.

The bluffs, and oft' the rocky ledge,
Bathed their feet in the water's edge;
The pines, like ship masts, towering tall,
The hills built up like ancient walls,
The mighty forest, ages old,
Arched the stream o'er many a hole,
And Nature, grand in her display,
Still claimed her own that early day.

The night was dark, 'twas understood,
But doubly dark when in the wood;
But we were fishing 'long the coast,
And had no time to look for ghosts,
And no one dared to mention dread
Of panthers in the trees o'erhead;

9

But, like the dread torpedo's shock,
A scream re-echoed from a rock

Which hung its ledge high o'er the stream,
To which our light had thrown a gleam;
That hideous scream, that wild hiss squall,
Raised hair on end, and hats grew tall;
And I can never paint the sound,
As down it poured and echoed round,
But surely I shall ne'er forget—
It seems just now I hear it yet.

But this enough to fill our cup;
We then explored no further up;
We now went trailing down the stream,
When Harry raised a maniac scream,
And little music for his dance,
A scream, a prance, a maniac glance;
And all the words we heard him say.
"Take it away! Take it away!

"It's cold as ice, and I shall die!"
And these words ended Harry's cry;
A huge green frog leaped from his throat,
Had squeezed 'neath collar of his coat,
And when he jumped he gave a squeal,
And Harry staggered back and reeled;
He climbed his leg beneath his clothes,
And scratched the skin from feet to nose.

All were scared, all in a flurry,
Frog made passage in a hurry;
And Harry, gasping, pale as death,
And wildly struggling for his breath,
And we, recovering from the shock,
Recalled the scream poured from the rock.
Well, Harry lived, boys laughed and screamed,
But all went gliding from the stream.

A Ramble O'er My Native Hills.

Long years have come and rolled away,
Since here we roamed in boyhood days,
When forest birds sang full and strong
In sweeter notes than human song.
From this high peak, so calm and still,
I trace the brook and distant hill,
Where ancient oaks our father slew,
When these dark woods to whites were new.

His axe was first in all the vale
When foot-prints marked the only trail,
When routes were blazed for men to see,
By chip or hack, from tree to tree.
High on this mountain peak I stand,
To scan again my native land,
More dearly prized than fame or gold,
Or even friends we loved of old.

Afar in yonder distant vale
The soundings of the muffled flail
Went out on wings of early morn
As well-timed music from the barn.
The golden wheat sent down to mill
Where burrs were run by drowning wheel,

Made snow-white biscuit, soft and sweet,
Which comes alone from new-grown wheat.

The woodlands fringed around the plain,
Where browning fields were minus grain;
The meadows, dressed in velvet green,
With scythe-mown stacks to dot the scene;
The lark had led her brood away,
Then sought a pinnacle of hay
To blend her music with the quail
That whistling stood upon a rail.

Unfading as the sun's sharp ray
Are sounds and scenes of that bright day;
Two miles away the woodland bell
Banged softly, yet we knew it well,
And all the herds in woods around
Were known by bells of different sounds;
And, oh! that sweetly singing bird,
Where oft in woods we found the herd.

Its notes were charming, clear and shrill,
And rang in woods from hill to hill;
How often did I hear that song
When hilltop shades were growing long
And gold-tint clouds on summer eve
In fleecy trains rolled on the breeze,
And in this golden leafy bower
Was e'er its home in childhood hour,

When hills were draped in green and gold,
To charm the heart in days of old;
Swamp-robin is our songster's name,
With all her music never tame;
She flits away sweet songs to sing,
You see her only on the wing.
But hark! she comes with sweeter tone
Than e'er in youth was ever known.

My cup is full, I ask no more,
I've scanned the scenes of childhood o'er,
And on this towering woodland hill
Our hidden champion singeth still.

Thus Nature bound her golden chains
 Around my boyish heart,
And evermore, while life remains,
 These charms can ne'er depart.

Shipwreck.

The mighty deep was deathly still,
   All 'round the sky rests on the sea;
Our pilot drove his ship at will,
   The sailors, sunning, lie at ease;
But soon we saw a drifting storm,
   And howling thunders loudly rolled,
The heaving clouds were rent and torn
   By flash and streaks like liquid gold.

The sleeping sea awoke in fright,
   And, angry, lashed her sheets to foam;
She rolled her waves to mountain height,
   And wrapped the ocean all in gloom ·
The heavens grew as black as night,
   The ship was tossed by wind and waves,
Still drifting, drifting to the right,
   Abreast the isle of sailors' graves.

The last bright hope had taken flight,
   The rigging torn from stem to stern,
The steam blew out with roar and might,
   The brilliant lamps refused to burn;
The waves had gone high o'er the deck,
   And sunk our helpless vessel low,

Which rose to meet a fearful wreck
 On cliffs where foam drifts white as snow.

Our ship was tossed upon a rock,
 A shivered wreck on stony bed,
While some recovered from the shock,
 Still others missing—they were dead.
We drifted there upon the isle,
 The long ill-fated isle of gloom,
Where ships lay mouldering all the while,
 And death was but the sailor's doom.

There human bones lie on the sands,
 The ship's tall masts had crumbled down,
Large diamond rings on skeleton hands,
 And trunks of gold were scattered round;
A safe there stood with open door,
 Large drawers filled with specie gold;
The inner safe ten thousand more
 Large diamonds, from the land of old.

Large steel-bound trunks of silver-ware,
 And costly watches made of gold,
And diamond bracelets sealed from air,
 Were packed with skill just from the mold.
But, oh! how small did all appear;
 The star of hope forever set,
The close of life then drawing near,
 The doom of others to be met.

Three suns had set o'er western seas,
    When, lo! just at the dawn of day,
A sail came driving on the breeze
    Toward the isle, though far away;
No ship had ever reached that shore,
    Save those by fearful storm and wreck;
Small boats were sent by sail and oar
    To bear the lost upon the deck.

The change was all this world could give,
    'T was simply raising from the dead,
That we again should drink and live,
    Where nature's bounty should be spread;
How small does all this world appear,
    When close of life is drawing near;
One hope is of ten thousand fold
    More value than a world of gold.

A Man from the Planet Venus.

A Brongole Kell from Venus Star
   Had sailed beyond its boundary line,
Attraction lost the man of air
   Was minus power to confine:
So like a boulder through all space
   He dropped toward this rolling world,
But miles above his resting place,
   The Brongole sails again unfurled.

Yet far above the sea and land
   This aged man, just from the star,
Beheld the world so broad and grand,
   With golden clouds hung in the air.
He lowered his Brongole on a hill
   O'erlooking all the city crowd,
There rushing to and fro at will,
   Like winds disturb the heaving cloud.

He could not dare to venture there,
   In all that hurly-burly crowd;
He put his Brongole in the air,
   And sailed away amid the cloud,
And then o'er hill and widening vale,
   He sailed upon the gentle breeze;

He saw the engine on the rail;
  The ships and boats upon the seas.

And all the world was on the fly,
  A rush! a clash! a roar of steam!
Till night shut out the golden sky,
  And twinkling stars began to gleam;
The cities burnt ten thousand lights,
  And ghostly shadows walked the streets;
The bell of time marked hours of night;
  Tall steeples waved their national sheets.

He sailed high o'er the city street,
  And lowered his Brongole on a hill,
Where men of note he chanced to meet,
  And this strange story did reveal:
A king there sat in golden chair,
  His kell around him in a fold;
His eyes were bright, but silvery hair,
  And he in years nine hundred old.

His wond'rous scenes of day had closed
  With golden tints of sunset sky;
And sad was he to learn our woes,
  And know that we were born to die.
A tear stole from the stranger's eye,
  When he these burning words were told,
That he on earth must surely die,
  For we of death have no control.

"O, my dear sir, I'm from you star,
   And I'm in years nine hundred old;
I cannot die in lands afar.
   For half my days can ne'er be told.
Our world is bright as noon-day sun,
   A world where pleasure never dies:
Each day new pleasures, just begun,
   Re-echoes gladness to the skies.

"Our days are bright, our nights are clear,
   No cloud can ever dim the sky;
But silvery gleamings fill the air,
   Sweeping grandeur from on high.
Ten thousand Brongoles swiftly fly,
   Ten thousand voices sweetly sing,
Ten thousand harps float through the sky,
   With thrilling music, on the wing.

"In yonder star there is no sin,
   No pain nor death can ever come;
As time rolls on, new life begins
   To perfect life where'er we roam;
There crystal streams forever flow,
   And ripple o'er the golden sands,
And trees of life spontaneous grow
   In balmy plains throughout the land.

"There cities stand aglow in white,
   With streets and walks of silvery pearl,

And golden chandeliers of light
  Hung in the skies all round the world;
And through the fields of boundless air,
  Upon the glittering winged Brongole,
We sail around a world so fair
  That eyes of earth could not behold.

"On gentle breeze the rich perfume
  Is wafted o'er the land and seas,
And all the world perpetual bloom
  Throughout that paradise of ease."
He put his Brongole in the air,
  On outspread wings of glittering gold,
And sailed beyond this world of care,
  With scenes too grand for earth to hold.

Thunder.

God heralds the lightning through the cloud,
In tremulous tones and rolling loud;
Rolls on and strikes the ethereal bell,
To ring the world's great funeral knell.

The sun goes down like liquid gold,
The cloud lifts up, and man beholds
God's glory painted on the sky,
Reflecting from the throne on high.

MRS. EMILY R. DAVIS.

My Long-Forgotten Friend, Lenore.

[Dedicated to My Wife.]

I met her when the evening train
    Came rolling from the highland wild.
I loved her.   I could not refrain,
    Yet had not seen her since a child.
When last we met 'twas close of school,
    In the grand Exhibition Hall,
When she was only ten years old,
    Yet wore a charm for one and all.

Six years had passed, she was full grown,
    And robed in beauty, angel fair.
I could not call this heart my own,
    When with a smile she met me there.
The train drew up.   We all aboard,
    Went gliding from each mountain bend,
'Twas then she dropped the careless word
    By which I knew she was my friend.

We met again in after days ;
    I loved her still, 'twas very true,
For she was lovely in her ways,
    And all respect to her was due ;

10

But half my heart belonged to one
  Whom I loved dearly long before,
But thought perhaps her heart was gone,
  And I could win it back no more.

For months had passed since last we met,
  And then I dreamed she loved no more.
I tried to doubt her and forget,
  But still I loved as ne'er before.
She then was nineteen summers old,
  And when we met love's cup was filled,
For I those smiles could then behold,
  And read in them she loved me still.

'Twas not a word that she had spoke ;
  'Twas not a sigh, 'twas not a tear ;
But in those eyes a tender look ;
  I knew she loved me, loved me dear.
By magnet power love's golden chain
  Entwined my long divided heart,
And by a pledge was bound the twain
  Through life to never, never part.

So years rolled on (fifteen or more),
  Till old school-mates were near forgot,
When in a dream I saw Lenore
  Where last we met, or near that spot.
Oh! long-forgotten friend, Lenore,
  Hast thou no friend to soothe thy way ?

" Oh, no," said she, " but ask no more,
  And call on me another day."

My heart grew sad, though all a dream,
  For still these words I pondered o'er,
And still could see her by the stream,
  Where oft we strolled long years before.
I dropped a note to friend Lenore,
  And soon received a kind reply.
She wished to have me call once more ;
  She knew that she must shortly die.

Oh, surely 'twas not all a dream ;
  So I at once resolved to go,
And soon I walked beside the stream
  Where in my dream I knew her woe.
She met me at her father's door,
  With joy expressed in every smile;
But ah ! 'twas not the once Lenore,
  Yet beauty lingered all the while.

And with a smile of calm repose
  She then referred to days of yore,
Of youth's bright hope and cloud of woes,
  And then she paused and said no more.
And when the hour for evening train,
  As we stood by the cottage door,
She asked me to return again,
  But a long farewell to friend Lenore.

Consolation.

"Then He arose, and rebuked the wind, and the raging of the water; and they ceased, and there was a calm."—*Luke viii. 24.*

Oh, the Saviour speaks to me!
  Lo! He walks upon the deep;
Now He stills the troubled sea,
  At His will the billows sleep.

CHORUS.—We are sailing on life's sea,
      Soon we'll reach the golden shore;
    Then, through all eternity,
      We shall praise Thee evermore.

Saviour, by thy grace divine
  We escape the tempter's snare;
Precious Jesus, we are Thine;
  Wilt Thou hear our humble prayer?

      CHO.—We are sailing, &c.

We have pushed from off the shore,
  Now to sail upon life's sea;
May Thy spirit guide the oar,
  For our strength must come from Thee.

      CHO.—We are sailing, &c.

Oh, we praise Thy holy name,
  For the palm of victory,
For the Lamb of Calvary slain,
  That from death we might be free.

    Cho.—We are sailing, &c.

We are coming to Thy bar,
  Dear Lamb of Calvary;
Faith beholds Thy glories there,
  And a crown laid up for me.

    Cho.—We are sailing, &c.

The Store.

In years past, thirty-two and more,
My dreams led out to run a store;
And now, for thirty years and more,
By day and night I've tramped the floor.

I then was young, now old and gray;
Time like a dream has passed away,
Some pages dark, some bright as day,
With valued friends to cheer the way.

High on the shelf old ledgers pile
Which fed on day-book all the while,
To mark the sales of city style
For ladies, girls and baby child.

Dishonest nature's own display
Has left its index day by day,
And strong bound ledgers stacked away
Record the names who do not pay.

Pen-holder brass, but pen-point gold,
The brass worn through where fingers hold
To charge the goods thus bought and sold,
To rich and poor, to young and old.

The walnut desk is long on hand,
Old show case on new counter stand,
New store-room finished nice and grand,
I now must leave to till the land.

Friends, rich and poor, we hang the oar
Upon the shore.   To run the store
'Haps nevermore.   The farm look o'er,
By rake and mower.   And timothy sower.

Oh! Shall We Meet on Heaven's Shore?

[Presented to My Sister, Mrs. V. Langfitte.]

Oh! shall we meet on heaven's shore
Those loved ones who have gone before?
My mother's star has never set,
Its beauty shines around me yet.

The harvest fields once brown and gold,
There father reap'd in ages old.
Alas! his sickle falls no more ;
Oh! shall we meet on that bright shore?

A brother, who had scarce known pain,
Stood like a stalk of well-formed grain;
Death's angel dipped his icy wing,
And friendly hearts bled from the sting.

A sister, with bright golden hair,
A brother, bent with age and care,
A host of friends, long since passed o'er ;
Oh! shall we meet on that bright shore?

A charming schoolmate, justly dear,
Robed in her beauty, angel fair,
Blooming in life's path like the rose
That graces the stem on which it grows.

Alas! the reaper's sickle fell;
Alas! a mournful funeral knell;
Alas! my friend was seen no more;
Oh! shall we meet on that bright shore?

I had a niece, with golden hair,
And all who knew her loved her dear;
At noon of life I saw her fade,
And on her cheeks a rose was laid,

Which bloomed beneath the ringlets gold,
Too charming fair for earth to hold.
We see that sweet bright face no more;
Oh! shall we meet on that bright shore?

No tearless eye could view that face
. When death had closed her cheerful eyes;
Alas! she slept with all her grace,
As though death's veil were mere diguise.

Mount of the Holy Cross.

Towering high in the western sky,
　　Stands the Mount of the Holy Cross;
And on this peak the cross so high,
　　Stands like the world's diadem lost,
Sculptured in traces bold and grand,
　　In ages dark and all unknown,
By Him who worketh not by hand,
　　Yet set the eternal cross of stone.

Set on this mount in silvery gray,
　　Wrapped the golden sunset cloud,
Unveiling at the dawn of day,
　　With diamonds glitter grand and proud.
On arms outspread the early morn
　　Pours golden splendor from the sun,
And all the ages yet unborn
　　Shall find its course is never run.

High on this pinnacle of stone,
　　The kingly mountain of the world,
There God has set His earthly throne,
　　The Cross, His banner, there unfurled.
The Golden Gate now stands ajar,
　　Men from the east are drifting by,

And rays gleam from the golden star,
   Which leadeth to that Cross on high.

The Cross of Calvary is lost;
   But Christ now sits upon the throne,
Pleads for a world of sin and dross,
   And points it to the cross of stone.
The unbelieving sinners, all,
   The Cross of Calvary disown;
Then gaze upon the mount so tall,
   And tremble 'neath the cross of stone,

Which from pure ether grandly shines,
   To prove the holy written word,
And on this seal the hand divine
   Has written, "Holy is the Lord."
Over the range to the Golden Gate,
   In splendor shines this living cross;
In sight of all men, small and great,
   The symbol of the sacred loss.

O, Sinner, Turn!

O, Sinner, turn! why will you die,
   And lose a precious soul?
When there's a mainsion built on high,
   Where streets are paved with gold.

Our Saviour, who on Calvary died,
   Stands ready to receive;
His arms of love extended wide,
   And bids thee now believe.

He died that sinful dust might live,
   And do we count the cost,
Or will we souls to Satan give,
   Regardless of the loss?

How bright the King of Glory shines,
   When sorrowing souls believe,
Who hear the whisper, thou art Mine,
   From sin thy soul is freed.

The cloud of darkness is removed;
   Bright heaven shines around,
And fills the soul with sacred love,
   And fits it for the crown.

The saints rejoice in Heaven above,
　While angels hover o'er,
The new-born soul, so full of love,
　Whose God they all adore.

Why will you, then, poor sinner, stay?
　Salvation's offered free;
And God invites, while friends do pray,
　And this is all for thee.

Colorado.

The world of nations have their kings,
 Where golden diadems glitter proud;
The King of States new glory brings,
 With crowning head high in the cloud.
Colorado is the King of States,
 With crowns of gold wrapped in the sky,
And from her walls the Golden Gate
 Is hinged on silver gleaming high.

Her mountain peaks are fringed with gold
 Her walls are knit with silver strands,
And silver brick just from the mold
 Are piled on pavements through the land.
Her snow-capped peaks of purity
 Send health and long life through the vale,
And ages of obscurity
 Are now the ages of the rail.

With windings through the walls so tall,
 And grading up the mountain side,
With power and room for one and all,
 Who on the rail may wish to ride;
Over the range they puff and blow,
 Ten thousand feet up in the sky,

Pass all the clouds which drift below,
   And wrap in golden clouds on high.

Tornado storms, in smutty sheet,
   Swift howl around the peak so high,
But dip their wings beneath the feet
   Of those who may be on the fly.
The golden rays flash from the sun,
   As nature sinks it down to rest,
And when its course is fully run,
   All heaven is golden in the west.

The King of States, and king of all,
   With tallest peaks e'er crowned with gold,
And deeper gorges, higher walls
   Than crown the Switzerland of old.
Fertile valleys, crystal fountains,
   And many wide extending plains,
Spread between her snow-capped mountains.
   Checkered with railroads and sweeping trains.

The Deer Chase.

The rolling hills were capped with snow,
And deer were rambling high and low,
A thunder's roar, 'mid timbers tall,
When hunters fired the one-ounce ball,
A wounded deer had given chase,
And not a man about the place.

So mother took her curs and knife,
To give the deer one chase for life;
The hills re-echoed music sounds,
All different sounds from many hounds,
And louder, louder came the sounds,
As forest hills they circled round.

But centering to the crossing place,
Where curs had often won the race,
Still louder bawled the trailing hound,
And lo! the deer came bouncing round,
Came loping, loping through the field,
Where mother had her curs concealed.

She loosed the chain, they scaled around,
They seized and tore him to the ground;
She cut his throat, and stopped the sounds

Of many yelping, yelping hounds.
And o'er yond hill and through that vale
The hounds came yelping on the trail.

And lo! a deer, with horns so tall,
Could whip the trail hounds, curs and all;
Then brother and I down, down the vale;
The fight was up, he seized a rail,
And with the vengeance of a fiend,
He struck his horns; his eyes turned green—

And with more madness than before,
He used his horns to plunge and gore.
Now all the dogs put in the chase,
By this dread moment reached the place;
But he was champion over all,
Eyes flashing green and horns so tall.

Then brother rallied with his rail,
His horns were splintered in his trail,
And he came tumbling with a bawl,
The dogs then seized him, one and all.
Oh, could I live it o'er again,
And hear the music of that train!

Long stretched across the hill and vale,
All yelping, yelping on the trail.
Now this recalls another scene,
When summer spread her carpet green;

A smaller deer had given chase
O'er field and fence, through father's place,

The dogs were nipping at her heels,
'T was near the house just in the fields;
I had two sisters there alone,
But to the field they bravely ran.
They reached the spot, the deer was down,
And, in excitement, now said one:

" Oh, cut its throat!   Be quick! be quick!"
She cut across, then tried to stick;
But, oh! the deer began to bawl,
She ran and screamed, climbed fences tall,
And threw the bloody knife away,
And lost her courage to this day.

Good Seed.

[Presented to Mrs. John Booth.]

Good seed sown on the earth
Shall ever bloom in heaven;
And while eternity rolls on
Grow more beautiful and lovely,
Variegating its tints
With the golden skies
Of the heavenly world,
While the everlasting fountain,
Which flows from the throne of God,
Shall lift its golden spray
In heavenly clouds,
To fall like dew-drops
On the never withering bloom
Which shall live forever and ever.

Lazy John.

I met Miss Lily in the rain;
  Her cheeks were fair and bright,
And Cupid's arrow caused a pain—
  I loved her dear at sight.

She smiled a little as we passed;
  My heart could not refrain,
I loved her first, I loved her last,
  I loved her in the rain.

I met Miss Lily's mother, then,
  Her friendship wished to gain;
I told her I was Lily's friend,
  I met her in the rain.

She gave a look I'll ne'er forget;
  "Do you mean to offend?
I fear, dear sir, you're too much set;
  Such rain-beau is no friend."

Christian Soldiers.

We're a band of Christian soldiers,
  Now enlisted for the war ;
On the wheels of time are rolling
  To the land of light afar ;
We shall fear no cannon's rattle,
  For our banner is unfurled,
And our General rules the battle
  Through the nations of the world.

CHORUS.

Then march along, happy throng—make no delay ;
Call those by the wayside while it's called to-day ;
Go tell them we are soldiers fighting for the Lord,
And if they join our army they shall have the great reward.

Yes, the teachers are our captains,
  And the school an army strong ;
Though our foe's arrayed in battle,
  Yet we fearless march along ;
And we'll say to heathen nations,
  Come and join our army, too,
For this land is not our station,
  But we have a land in view.

CHO.—Then march along, &c.

From the heathen land of China
　To the wilds of Afric's plain,
And through hills and vales of Syria,
　We should lengthen out our chain;
By the mission work our army
　May unfold her banners there,
And the heathen souls of darkness
　May unite with us in prayer.

　　　Cho.—Then march along, &c.

Then awake, O ye that slumber!
　Be ye always at your post,
And we'll swell this happy number,
　Seeking Heaven's boundless coast;
For our home's beyond the river,
　Where no sorrows ever come;
In that long and bright forever
　We shall rest with Christ at home.

　　　Cho.—Then march along, &c.

A Happy Dream.

In shades of night a happy dream
  Once led me back to youthful days;
And in the ball-room beauty seemed
  To flash with smiles and grand displays.
A cousin there I gladly met,
  With blooming cheeks and sparkling eyes;
A tender glance, expression sweet,
  And love which from all innocence rise.

And we of course have not grown old;
  We've simply slept thirty-five years;
The love we knew has not grown cold,
  But wakes with joy and loving tears.
She meets me with a loving smile,
  We dance as oft we danced before;
We love, but not in cupid's style—
  To meet the Parson on the floor.

Yet we are single all the while,
  And talk of those we love so dear;
And have no secrets of a style
  Too good for each other to hear;
And so we turn the golden page.
  And there we find a written line;

"To my beloved I'm engaged;"
  "And so," says she, "I am to mine."

So at this little secret glance
  We both are more than happy still,
The floor much softer for the dance,
  The music carries us at will;
But we would gladly leave the floor
  And talk of prospects sure and bright,
When we should push from off the shore
  With double oar and boat so light.

But, that fair angel, whom I loved,
  Had winged away to some bright shore,
And in the happy crowd I moved,
  Was still alone, while on the floor.
My hope was bright that we should meet
  On some fair shore of wedded bliss,
Where golden sands might pave her street,
  And lips should meet no parting kiss.

I then stepped back from out the dream;
  My heart was beating quick and warm:
The embers cast a timid gleam;
  My angel's wing wrapped round my arm.
The sands of life had rolled away,
  The years that stopped were in the dream:
They'd left their trail of silvery gray,
  In them my cousin had not seen.

This World's Riches.

You may boast of your mountains,
  Your valleys behold;
Of your herds and your fountains,
  Your silver and gold;
Of your million-built hall,
  Your cars on the rail,
Your monuments tall,
  Your vessels on sail.

Of your factory and mill,
  Your cities and town,
Your gold in the hills,
  Where riches abound;
Of the smooth, fertile plains,
  Which spread in the West,
And imagine all gains
  As riches and rest.

But 'tis all vain delusion;
  Each gem has a snare,
A fear of intrusion,
  A sting or a care;
For the only true wealth
  This world can define.
With a share of good health,
  Is contentment of mind.

The Lonesome Chief.

In days gone by, long years ago,
  A little crew sought for this land;
Their vessel sailed for weal or woe,
  Yet enterprise was great and grand;
And lo! they found the gloomy shore,
  The home of unknŏwn savage man,
Which the dark forest clustered o'er
  From western gulfs to eastern sand.

'Twas when the little winding streams,
  In lonesome murmurs, found their way
Through shady groves, where sunlight beams
  Had never poured their golden ray;
And when the song of spring-time birds
  Were only heard by savage man,
And when wild beasts, in groups and herds,
  Were chased by yelling Indian bands.

The chief then bartered with the whites,
  And sold his birthright for a bribe;
Released to them his forest rights,
  To seek the West with all his tribe;
They roamed the Mississippi wild,
  Exposed to death by winter's blast;

Their chief survived with but his child,
　Who drooped in spring and died at last.

When he had hollowed out the bed
　That soon must hide that lovely face,
He gazed upon the sleeping dead,
　The fairest bloom of all his race,
Then kissed and laid her in the tomb ;
　She was his last and only friend ;
And then he thought of childhood home
　And what must shortly be his end.

Again he sought the sea-wave home,
　The home his father's birthright gave,
And there in tattered rags he roamed,
　Where once he sported with the brave ;
And then, with bitterness of soul,
　His last and loud complaints were made,
While standing 'neath the oaks of old,
　Where wigwam beds in youth were laid :

"You drove me from my native wild,
　And slew the forest that I loved,
And now my wife and only child
　Camp in yon moon, 'mid stars above ;
And I, with burning tears, now stand
　To view my childhood's landscape o'er,
Where all my tribe went heart and hand
　When first I knew this forest shore.

"You drove us from yon seaside wave,
    That beautiful and lovely sea;
You drove us to the icy grave,
    Where all have sipped death's cup but me;
And soon I too must follow on,
    To scale the hills of yonder moon,
Which is our destined hunting-ground;
    There all must greet old chieftain soon."

MISS LENO BELLE.

[174]

Leno Belle.

[Dedicated to her brother, Hon. William Jeffrey.]

The sun swept o'er hills far away,
    And morning splendor, bright as gold,
Then painted nature with display
    Far as the eye can e'er behold;
The silvery dew-drops kissed the rose,
    Then slyly stole within its fold
To wake it from its sweet repose
    And variegate with rainbow gold.

The birds sang sweetly in the trees,
    And mournfully complained the dove—
One representing life and ease,
    One representing loss of love;
All mingling sounds and lovely scenes
    Refreshed the shades on memory's wall,
When school of youth was ever green,
    And Belle wore charms for one and all.

Alone I stood amid the tombs,
    Where sods were turned years long ago;
The heaping turf beneath the bloom
    Inclosed the sleeping dust below;

I read each stone with lifted head,
  Which bore each name in letters small;
But one I sought among the dead,
  Just one alone, and that was all.

My search was long and seemed in vain,
  And I had changed my course to go;
Unconscious steps led back again,
  Ah! why it was I do not know;
Impressions more than words could speak
  Then led me to a distant stone,
And thus the name I there would seek
  Mysteriously to me was shown.

What fairy hand had led me there,
  Ah! I can never tell;
But 'twas the name of the once fair
  In school, the charming Leno Belle;
And though the flight of time had marked
  Three years upon her lonely grave,
And sealed that form deep in the dark,
  Yet left a pang for beauty's slave.

Eclipse of the Sun, August 7, 1869.

The sun now hung a golden fringe,
  Around the edges of the moon,
And cast a shadow dark and dinge
  When shades of night were not in tune.

The stars looked through a gauzy veil,
  Dim shadows walked like ghosts at night.
And darkness spread o'er hill and dale;
  The heavens burnt a hidden light.

The earth grew strangely pale and faint,
  The trees wore robes of millet-green,
The hills wore crowns like tints of paint,
  The rich-clad valleys trailed between,

The birds now sung their evening song,
  The chickens bid the day good-bye.
The night-owl hooted gruff and strong,
  Because the moon was in the sky.

But soon swept on a daybreak scene;
  The fowls and birds saw their mistake;
The earth awoke and dressed in green,
  The stars went out, 'twas then daybreak.

The owl went back to bed again,
The rooster blew his daybreak horn,
The birds sang sweet o'er hill and glen,
And three P. M. was then the morn.

Mr. Wm. F. Davis, the warrior referred to in the following poem, was the father of the writer. He served in the War 1812, in the command of General Harrison.

The Warrior's Forest Home.

[Dedicated to President Harrison.]

The deathly clash of war had ceased,
  The Britain boys had left the shore;
The boys of '12 were all released,
  The cannon's belch was heard no more,
A soldier left the stage of war
  To seek a home 'mid forest gloom,
Where oaks eclipsed the morning star,
  And savage beasts had made their home.

A wild romantic woodland scene,
  Where crystal waters murmured low,
And mountain peaks were ever green
  Through autumn days and winter's snow.
No mark of skill in all that land,
  No woodsman knew the winding stream,
But shadows fell so thick and grand,
  The scene was more a fairy dream.

That valley was the panther's home,
　And once the red man's hunting ground,
Where squaws and warriors used to roam,
　And where their weapons still are found.
There elk and deer, wild cats and bear,
　Grey fox and wolves were found;
The mink, the otter, coon and hare,
　Red fox and squirrel, also abound.

And yet that lone ax-stroke was heard,
　And giant oaks fell to the ground,
And soon a cabin-hut was reared
　Amid the gloom that hung around.
The warrior, with his deathly gun,
　Re-echoed thunder through that land;
But still the wolves refused to run
　Until they saw the fiery brand.

With hideous howls they oft would come,
　When sheep were in their rugged pen,
And force the dogs to seek a home,
　Then storm the fort within the glen.
The old cock blew his daybreak horn,
　The hoot-owl heard his homespun note,
And then away, in early morn,
　To seize and cut the stranger's throat.

But soon the varmints' grand retreat
　Were rolling fields of golden grain,

And garden beds were blooming sweet
  Where giant oaks had just been slain.
Though first to mark and pave the way
  In all that lonely vale of gloom,
That warrior lived, when old and gray,
  And still that spot was then his home.

'T was my dear home in childhood's day;
  There sweetly sung the lark at dawn,
When all the fields were green in May,
  And frogs were croaking in the pond.
The pheasant hid within the vale,
  And bravely beat his morning drum;
While in the stubble perched the quail
  That whistled round my cottage home.

How dear those childhood scenes are now—
  The old gnarled oak, the grassy field,
The orchard 'neath the mountain brow,
  The little brook and shady mill,
The barn, the crib, the mossy well,
  The cottage home, the crystal stream,
The song of birds, the distant bell—
  Now seems as but a placid dream.

In Heaven we Shall See Them.

[Two children of the author, Ida V. and Emerson B.]

A beauteous child was IDA V.,
    Whose dust now in the grave-yard lies;
Her rosy cheeks were fair to see,
    And bright as stars her dark blue eyes,
And softly curled her golden hair,
    Like gilded clouds in distant skies;
But sadly now her vacant chair
    Stands empty, since its owner dies.

Like music soft, we heard her voice,
    Like angel fair, we saw her form
In childish play and sport rejoice;
    Alas! from us too soon she's torn.
Oh! could we see that dimpled hand,
    Those pleading looks, which haunt us still,
As she asked her mamma, from the pan
    Her little painted cup to fill.

Where are the toys with which she played,
    Where are her little hat and dress?
Her toys are in the drawer laid,
    With hat and shoes, and all the rest.
I know for her we shall not weep,
    For doubtless she has gone to rest;

Her soul in silence doth not sleep—
　God called her home, He thought it best.

Again, a dark and lonely night,
　When earth and air were hushed and still,
In shades of gloom and dim moonlight,
　Again death's cup for us was filled.
Around the snow-white couch we stood,
　And watched the cheeks in death turn pale,
And tried in vain to give relief,
　And call him back from out the vale.

A lovely boy, two summers' old,
　Then passed from us and earth away;
How soon the treasures which we hold,
　Slip from our grasp, and seek decay!
But faith beholds these loved ones fair,
　Those Jewels which our hearts have worn,
Transformed into a lovely pair
　Of angels, near the Father's throne.

It sees them walk the gold-paved streets,
　In robes of glory, hand in hand,
And, with the sainted ones, there meet
　Who long before passed to that land.
It sees their glory-gilded wings,
　Their golden harps and starry crowns,
And hears the peaceful songs they sing,
　Where toil and pain no more are found.

Autumn Days.

[Dedicated to My Youngest Daughter, ETHEL.]

["Oh! sing to me of Autumn days,
　The crowning beauties of the year,
Where eyes can feast upon the haze
　Of gold and crimson, green and sear."]

How can we sing of Autumn days,
　When Nature robes herself to die,
Though beauty crowns the morning rays,
　And gold-tipped mountains kiss the sky?

But who could sing of beauty now,
　Without a sadness in the soul?
When hills must fade from foot to brow,
　And dross replenish crowns of gold.

True, beauty lingers on each hill,
　And fills the soul with pure delight;
But there's a thought, far deeper still:
　The brightest ray must end in night.

The crimson hills and mountains high,
　With tints of gold and blendings green,
The painter's art do all defy—
　'Twould blush to even sketch the scene.

But Nature has an artist old,
  Who, with a finger's touch of snow,
He sprinkles earth and tints it gold,
  And paints the hills and valleys low,

But soon must all this blush of gold
  And fleecy robe, that touch the sky,
Fall at the feet of those of old,
  And Nature's beauty then must die.

The author of the above lines resides in the mountains of West Virginia, the scenery of which conduces to the lofty flights of sublime imagery. The soul is there ever thrilled by those scenes which superinduce poetry and oratory.—Tom Wash Smith, *in the Baltimore Herald.*

Payton's Ride.

[Dedicated to Mr. Tom Wash Smith, Editor of *The Baltimore Herald*]

Far up the stream a hero stood,
While crushing, rumbling, came the flood;
With steed at hand he mounted high,
Down, down the stream he raised the cry:
" Fly for your life! the flood is nigh!
The lake's death-wave is rolling high!"
On, on he rode, with fearless speed,
While frothing, foaming, flew his steed.

Swift on his track came rumbling sounds;
High on the waves came floating towns,
With living, dying, and the dead,
And shrieking, crying, on they sped.
The hero's horse, with swift-plied feet,
Flew wildly thro' the Johnstown streets;
" The dam has burst!" he loudly cried,
" And towns are floating on the tide!

" Fly for your life! the river's wrath
Is sweeping down a deadly path !"
And onward flew the hatless man;
" Fly for your life! the flood's at hand!"

The surging crowd rushed out to see
Who this wild maniac could be;
No one knew him, but some few fled,
While others, smiling, felt no dread.

A clash! a rush! a sullen roar!
Down on the town mad waters pour.
Strong buildings, like a flimsy shell,
Went crushing as the current fell,
And, in the twinkling of an eye,
A myriad victims, doomed to die,
Were struggling 'gainst the foaming wrath
Which swallowed all within its path.

Fine parlors, halls, and pleasant homes,
Were swept like chaff out on the foam.
Rich daughters grasped their bonds and chains,
And diamond rings, and life-time gains;
And lovely mothers, young and fair,
And aged ones, with silvery hair—
All struggling in the deathly waves
Which dealt no mercy for its slaves.

A rumbling roar, a grinding sound;
He turned his steed from ill-fate ground,
And urged him on for nearest hills—
But waves had crushed the town and mills,
And swept them on tornado speed,
And swallowed up the foaming steed.

Brave herald, horse, and all, went down
With ruins of the late Johnstown.

"God save the rider!" the people cried,
As he went flying down the tide.
The prayer was heard—the angry wave
Relaxed its grip, gave up the brave
Who risked his life to warn the town,
That they might flee, tho' he be drowned.
A nobler act, or famous deed,
Was never known on ship or steed.

America should stamp three crowns—
One for Sheridan, one for Collens Gray,
And one for Payton, who warned the towns
When a myriad souls were swept away.
Let history now record his name—
A Paul Revere, a hero brave,
Who caps the pinnacle of fame
By swift-plied feet before the wave.

Mr. Davis has a true harp somewhere in the reverberating valley of his mountain home. He writes poetry as naturally as a brook rolls along to a cascade, some of which will live when he has passed away. The fearless rider who carried the signal of danger to the innocent victims, all unconscious of impending woe, will go into history as imperishable as the unwritten law of human emotion. So long as the heart-beats count quicker numbers at the recital of deeds of daring, just so long will this herald of danger be on the tongue of thrilling stories, and that means forever, or as long as time knows her calendar. Mr. Davis gives out a hint which no doubt is in crayon sketches in many a studio in this broad domain, even while he writes of it. We do not have on our walls the portrait of any hero of ancient or modern times. We worship God, and not man or mammon. But when the painter gives us the picture of that messenger riding to his death, for aught he knew, that others might live, we want a copy of that man on the foaming steed, whose deep pathos is the strongest evidence of the heart that is filled with rapturous concern for the weal of others; and that interest is above estimate, for it is the affinity, or kinship, of man with his Maker, or as the theologian would tell you, the full corn in the ear.—Tom Wash Smith, *in The Baltimore Herald.*

["The Lonely Window" and "The Answer" is a portion of a play written by the author of this book, in which Mrs. Taylor Ward, (then about twenty-one years of age), represented "Nellie," and in which she showed remarkable talent for the stage. The writer of the play represented "Col. Whitaker;" "Nellie" and himself taking the leading parts, assisted by twenty-two ladies and gentlemen. The play represented the separation, the absence of three years, and the return.]

The Lonely Window.

[Dedicated to Mrs. Taylor Ward.]

By the lonely window sit I here
  And listen to the autumn sigh,
While shining hosts of stars so fair,
  Bedeck the soft ethereal sky ;
Their beauties call to mind again
  The absent friend, so dear to me,
Which fills my lonely heart with pain,
  And wafts my thoughts across the sea.

I watch the slowly setting sun,
  And hail with joy the morning ray,
Each moment nearing your return ;
  Thus time drags wearily away ;
And when alone I think of thee,
  And pray that God may spare your life,

And guide you safely back to me—
  Your lonely friend, your faithful wife.

And in the silent shades of night,
  When gilded moon shines soft and fair,
In some bright dream again take flight
  To China—for my heart is there.
But when I waken from my dream
  I find a lonely, vacant chair;
Oh! could I fly across the stream,
  How gladly would I meet you there.

THE ANSWER—SONG OF THE SHIPWRECK.

'Twas calm and still upon the sea,
  Blue skies without a cloud,
And all on board sang merrily
  While through the deep we plowed;
But soon we saw terrific clouds
  And vivid lightning flash;

'Neath thunder's howl the ocean bow'd,
  And waves began to splash;
Then midnight darkness
  Eclipsed the noonday sun,
While mountain waves came rolling back,
  And lo! our sails were gone.

But still we heard the thunder's roar
  Amid the wind-torn clouds,

While rain in torrents downward pour'd,
  And every knee was bow'd;
We sank beneath the rolling waves,
  Which swept our naked deck,
Then rose again, and all were saved,
  Though but a fearful wreck;
Then raging billows
  Swept us on the shore,
It seem'd that all the timbers broke
  Amid one crash and roar.

We drifted there upon the shore,
  When starving seem'd our doom,
It was an isle where long before
  A crew was left to roam;
Their bleaching bones were near the wreck,
  Their sails had crumbled down,
And just beneath the shattered deck
  Their pearls and gold were found.
Oh! horrid picture,
  Which hangs on that dread shore,
It seemed our doom was sure the same
  (Three hundred men or more).

For days we watched the rolling sea,
  With but scant rations drawn,
When lo! the flag of liberty
  Was seen in early dawn;

They were my faithful navy boys
　In search of our lost crew,
Whose hearts were glad and full of joy
　When near our wreck they drew.
Out on the ocean
　Again we quickly sailed,
With milk and wine our bowls to fill,
　While we rove through the gale.

We then returned to China's shore
　With gems which we had found
While on this isle, where long before
　A wreck was thrown aground.
But now my thoughts return to thee;
　Sure I would give my gold
To hear thee speak one word to me
　Or half thy charms behold.
Oh! dearest Nellie,
　Do not weep for me,
The time is short when I again
　Your lovely face shall see.

My dearest wife, weep not for me,
　My stay will soon be o'er,
Then I shall plow the rolling sea
　To my loved native shore.
I long to meet with you, my dear,
　Thy lovely features trace,

And wipe away the briny tears
That stealeth down thy face.
Then, dearest Nellie,
Do not weep for me,
My vessel soon shall plow again
The rough and rolling sea.

Dear Bessie of Ohio.

Now, boys and girls, this is for you,
And sure it is a story true,
The cause for it we could not tell—
Perhaps some owl knew very well.
'Twas night, and I accompanied late
Miss Bessie, of Ohio State.
Dear Bessie was a pretty girl,
I loved her best in all the world.

As I was young and knew no better,
And she disposed to chat still later,
My love grew deeper all the while—
For she was witty, and dressed in style—
And on her smiles she wore a charm,
Which plainly said she knew no harm;
So Cupid's arrow, first and last,
Had pierced my heart and bound it fast.

For hours the folks had gone to bed—
Her mother's room just over head—
The clock had marked the hour of ten,
When flying, squalling, came a hen,
Came dashing 'gainst the parlor door;
Then all was still, we heard no more;

A flying turkey thumped the wall,
And on the ground we heard it fall.

Another fell, thump! in the yard.
Her mother screamed, "Oh, my dear Lord!
For God's sake, Bessie, go and see
What all that clattering can be!"
Then flying guineas made such a noise,
Disturbed the slumber of the boys;
With lamp in hand they all came down,
Old lady in a long white gown.

Then Bessie, dear, to my surprise,
Hung her sweet hands close o'er my eyes;
But in the yard they hunted 'round,
And turkeys, chickens, guineas found;
Some were dead and some were dying,
Others squalling, others flying;
But, all in all, it was a time
I never told, but now, in ryhme.

But, as the ages creep along,
I place dear Bessie in my song,
And take a glimpse back in the past,
When loved her first and loved her last.
Did I go back, you mean to say?
Oh no! ne'er saw her from that day,
But often wished to be surprised
By her sweet hands hung o'er my eyes.

But then, perhaps, if we should meet,
The fowls might flutter at our feet,
A sacrificial offer make,
To mean their dying for our sake;
But let the cause be what it might,
The trouble came that fatal night,
And we took warning, there and then,
To never, never meet again.

Now, boys, this is a hint for you,
And sure it is a story true,
For Cupid's arrow, like a dart,
Goes piercing thro' the youthful heart,
But leaves behind a road of thorns,
Never stops and never warns,
But, like the story I have told,
Oft leaves its victims in the cold.

You know the welcome strains of our Highland friend, whose songs are so full of pathos and happy symphony. We wish he would write more frequently.—Tom Wash Smith, *in The Baltimore Herald.*

Centennial Years.

[Dedicated to My Son-in-Law, Attorney A. L. Taylor.]

As time moves on, from stage to stage,
　The great events of years gone by
Live in the heart of this great age
　As treasured gifts from God on high.
Centennial Year of Seventy-six
　Was crowned with arts from all the world,
And kings and statesmen intermixed
　'Neath freedom's flag, proudly unfurled.

And all the nations, far and near,
　Loaned helping hands to celebrate
Events of that Centennial Year
　Which formed the great United States.
Our flag, in years one hundred old,
　There waved o'er greatest skill on earth,
While kingly nations, grand and old,
　Were dross beside our nation's worth.

The Corliss, run by Fulton's steam,
　The nations spoke by Morse's wire;
Now Edison sends a wond'rous gleam
　More brilliant than the sun or fire.

The crown is due Columbia's land
  For use of steam and lightning wire,
The telephone, from Edison's hand,
  And city lights by friction fire.

The next in turn comes Eighty-Nine,
  The President Centennial Year,
Events of which may now remind
  The Revolutionary tear.
'Twas then the mighty hero came
  Who led the great victorious war—
He figured high in national fame
  To shield the flag which bore the stars.

He comes through towns ablaze with fire,
  His path is strewn with maiden's flowers,
Triumphant arches fringed on wire,
  In honor of the eventful hours.
He comes, the mighty Father comes,
  Vast armies crowd and cannons roar,
The way is cheered by fife and drum
  And armies that he led before.

He comes—he steps upon the stage,
  He takes the oath as Freedom's King,
Or Ruler, of that happy age
  When freedom's songs began to ring.
He comes—four million freemen stand
  To welcome him who victories won,

And severed Britain's iron band—
    He comes—and lo! 'tis WASHINGTON!

And now the Century Year is done;
    A sixty million nation hails
With pride the day its years begun,
    When Federal Hall the Chief unveiled.
From thence the national sky was clear,
    The ship, complete, launched on the seas,
And now she's sailed one hundred years,
    With victory crowning every breeze.

All hail! Columbia's Freedom hail!
    Let now another century run,
And may the ship stem every gale
    And warlike storm that clouds her sun,
Till kingly crowns shall rust and fall,
    And monarchs blush with national shame,
And may the Goddess grow so tall
    That all the world may see the flame.

Discovery of Elk Creek.

Through dreamy woods two hunters strolled,
    Where man had never trod before,
And through the forest, gray and old,
    A river bent around the shore;
And as they neared the silvery stream,
    They looked down thro' the mossy wood,
And in the centre of the scene
    A herd of forest cattle stood.

The woodsman fired: one, bleeding, fell;
    They slightly stirred, but no alarm,
Whence came the roar they could not tell,
    But never dreamed of slightest harm.
They knew not death by weapons small;
    They often heard the thunders roar,
And rumbling timbers as they fell—
    But deadly rifles, ne'er before.

Again they fired, and still they fell;
    They heard their bleeding comrades groan,
But how came death they could not tell,
    Yet all the herd was dead save one;
He shook his woolly mane and fled,
    Affrighted by the odious smell,

But circled round his bleeding dead :
　The woodsman fired, the seventh fell.

And then they neared the river's shore,
　Which bent its course thro' forests deep,
Where man had never roamed before,
　And all the forests seemed to sleep.
The timbers bent far o'er the stream,
　And clustered down the rustic shore,
The noon-day sun was but a gleam
　Through forest shades in streaks to pour.

"Hoo, hoo-hoo, hoo, wah!" cried the owl,
　Arousing from his sleepy den ;
The wolf had raised a hideous howl,
　The panther screamed at sight of men ;
Thousands of years those vales had slept,
　Yet murmuring rivers still had flown,
Bright Summer smiled and Winters swept
　O'er lands of mineral, oil and stone.

Son Billy.

When scorching fever seized my head,
  Son Billy kindly came to me,
He thought it was my dying bed,
  And he a farm could plainly see.
"Dear father, how are you?" he said;
  "Do you my aid or presence need?"
He knew of my unconscious head—
  He asked me then to make a deed.

I knew not what my hand had done
  Until my raging fever ceased;
Ah! soon my troubles then begun,
  And long adieu was bid to peace.
Son Billy came to me one day—
  'Twas at my quiet home of ease—
He told me there I could not stay,
  But pull my stakes and leave the keys.

I asked Son Billy what he meant,
  Thus driving me from friends and home?
"You have no means to pay your rent,
  So Tom, my son, has fixed to come."
I told Son Billy 'twas my home,
  That I should never, never go.

Said he, "My deed has sealed your doom,
    And I will shortly let you know."

I asked him what he meant by deed,
    When from his pocket he withdrew
A paper, and said, "Now take heed
    While I this writing read to you."
"My God!" said I, "is that my hand?"
    "Oh, yes," said Bill, "'tis even true."
"So you are owner of my land,
    And not a cent to me is due!"

I then revealed this to my wife,
    For she was old and feeble, too,
And had no means to sustain life,
    And not a cent to her was due;
But yet Son Billy drove us out
    To seek a home where'er we could;
We knew not how to go about
    To beg for lodging, clothes and food.

But friends then told us what to do:
    We sued Son Billy for our farm;
And then he said, "Now, as 'tis you,
    I'll feed and clothe you; fear no harm."
So Tom gave up our house again,
    And gladly we returned once more;
But Billy still kept all our land,
    And used us worse than e'er before.

For years we lived in sore distress,
  Half-clothed, half-fed; and Billy said
It cost too much to keep us dressed,
  And often wished we both were dead.
My wife was good and kind to me,
  Provided meals as best she could,
But tears would start sometimes at tea,
  When table scant before us stood.

At last wife's son, who knew the way
  Son Billy always treated us,
Came for my dear to go away,
  And rid her of the lasting fuss.
I could not say, " dear wife, don't go;"
  No, I preferred to die alone,
That we might not grieve Billy so
  To dig both graves and spare the room.

My life was spent a home to gain,
  But now, because my head is gray,
A bed of thorns to ease my pain,
  A frown, a curse, a rent to pay.
The heathen mobs respect gray hairs,
  The savage beasts have hearts within,
But aged parents, bent with cares,
  Are drove from home without a sin.

Kitty and the Mouse.

"Oh! ma, my little kitty
    To-day brought in a *mice*,
It never looked so pretty,
    And never played so nice.
The mouse would skip around,
    My kitty then would run
And box the fellow down,
    Yet did it all in fun.

"The mouse was swift to learn,
    And then it stood on end,
And tried to box in turn,
    Himself thus to defend.
I wish you'd seen it, ma,
    For it from end to end
Was less than kitty's paw,
    Yet ready to defend.

"I'm sure my kitty laughed,
    To see its tiny feet
Half-lifted, in behalf
    The fate it feared to meet.
Then mousey bounced around,
    And kitty boxed his tail,

But soon a hole was found,
 And mouse slipped Kitty's nail.

"Poor kitty looked so bad,
 I'm sure t'was almost sick,
But I was really glad
 The mouse had played the trick,
For cruel little kitty,
 It loves to skip and play,
And never stops to pity
 Whate'er should be its prey."

On Receiving Her Picture.

Alas! Earth's brightest gem is gone;
  And once again the tolling bell
For her was rung, so loud and long,
  The mountains echoed back farewell.

While sadness filled the dreamy air,
  And fields of nature seemed to mourn,
Because the belle of all the fair
  From earth and friends away was torn.

Alas! alas! she sleepeth now,
  Amid the tombs beneath the clay,
While golden locks bedeck the brow,
  So pale and fleeting fast away.

This mirrowed shadow of that form,
  Though sweetly fair, with ringlets gold,
Is but a feint of nature's charm,
  With eyes revealing love untold.

Oh, piercing eyes! my very soul
  Now shrinks beneath thy ardent gaze,
For all thy charms I still beheld,
  And read in them of gone-by days.

The days when Cupid's magic power
    Had stamped this image on my heart,
And in return that blissful hour,
    She took with me a lover's part.

Though lovers still were only friends,
    Yet of a stamp forever true,
But fate decrees and friendship ends,
    Still forms appear in brighter hue.

Lamentation.

[Dedicated to Mrs. Charley Hill, Gallipolis, Ohio,]

We often shed a burning tear
   When thinking o'er the past;
While friends so dear doth linger near,
   Sad thoughts come rushing fast.

Amid the thorny branch we find
   Sweet flowers fresh and gay;
So kindred friends, beloved and kind,
   Make bright the gloomy day.

There's something in a kindred love
   That words cannot express;
We feel this pang when dear ones leave—
   Bound for the " Golden West."

Yet, fated thus, it seems to be
   That friends most dear must part;
So chilling sighs are felt for thee,
   And sadness fills the heart.

That merry birds may sweetly sing,
   And flowers look fresh and gay;

Yet painful partings leave a sting
   For time to wear away.

The rose-tint cloud in beauty swells
   Beneath the starry gleam,
Then vanish, like that hope which tells
   Us pleasure's but a dream.

The American Eagle.

The nation's bird a home doth seek
　　Where craggy cliffs stand towering high,
And honors but the hoary peaks
　　That seem to kiss the distant sky;
And when she spreads her golden wings
　　To bear her onward through the gale,
She soars away beyond the ring
　　Of village bells throughout the vale,

This was her home when heathen gloom
　　Had run its course from sea to sea,
And nations dreamed there was no room
　　To plant a flag of liberty;
But sons of England plowed the wave
　　And pitched their tent in heathen lands,
While England followed to enslave,
　　And bound them with her iron bands.

In cabin homes for years they dwelt,
　　While bowing to the British crown;
Oppression sore long years they felt,
　　Till yielding place no more they found.
With one accord they boldly spoke,
　　And cried aloud for liberty;

Determined to throw off the yoke,
  And fighting, die, or else be free.

With Washington placed at the head,
  The father of our happy land,
The starry blue and eagle led
  That gallant little patriot band.
They saw old Britain's flashing steel,
  And heard the cannon's sullen roar;
Yet dashed they o'er the gory field
  With shouts of "Onward to the shore!"

The God of Victory crowned their blows,
  They drove them back o'er land and sea,
They humbled low our haughty foes
  And gave this land to liberty.
Thus brave and true, with numbers small,
  They drove the British from our shore
And raised our eagle banner tall,
  That here shall wave forevermore.

She led them through the cruel war
  To Victory's undying fame,
And then amid the thirteen stars
  She perched to rest and to remain,
May God forbid that she shall fall
  Disgracefully and lose her trust,
Or freedom's banner, shield of all,
  Be soiled or trampled in the dust.

For it protects brave freedom's land,
  The proudest nation in the world;
The States are knit by union band,
  And pledged to keep the stripes unfurled.
The roaring tide of wealth rolls on
  From State to State and sea to sea,
And as the sun crowns each new dawn
  New millions crown homes of the free.

We envy our poet friend; his home is soul-inspiring, and we can-not wonder that he should occasionally strike his harp with metres akin to immortal bards of sculptured fame.—Tom Wash Smith, *in The Baltimore Herald.*

'Tis My Only Kitty, Mother.

Tune—"Infant School."

Now is it not a pitty
    For a little child as I,
To send my little kitty
    Out in the cold to cry?

Chorus—Oh! I can't let it go
           Out in the cold and snow;
           I love my little kitty so
           I cannot let her go.

Oh! mother, please to let it be,
    It sings to me so sweet,
And in the morning you shall see
    It prance around my feet.

Cho.—Oh! I can't let it go, &c.

It lays its feet upon my breast
    And sleeps with me content.
Now, mother, how could kitty rest
    If in the snow it's sent?

Cho.—Oh! I can't let her go, &c.

You know that kitty catches mice
   Out 'neath the old barn floor,
Then skips along o'er snow and ice
   To reach my bed-room door.

Cho.—Oh! I can't let her go, &c.

Then cover up your kitty dear,
   I could not make it go,
And have my darling waste a tear
   For kitty in the snow.

Cho.—No, I can't make it go
    And grieve my darling so;
    You love your little kitty so
    I can't make it go.

I thank you now, my dearest mother,
   And kitty thanks you, too,
For it will sleep with me and brother
   While papa sleeps with you.

Cho.—For I can't let it go, &c.

Mystery.

[A scene on the Writer's Farm.]

A little brook, with beauties grand,
  Comes rippling from a mountain spring,
And winds its way o'er stone and sand
  Through woods where birds melodious sing.

Through time unknown to days of man,
  This murmuring stream has found its way,
And cut a ravine through the land,
  A link in nature's grand display.

And interwoven timber bends
  In wreathy arches o'er the walls,
Through which this little brook descends,
  To make its leap down o'er the falls.

It rushes down its winding stair,
  A bold and sparkling silvery sheet;
It sends its mist into the air,
  And forms a rainbow at its feet.

By little streams the chasm cliff
  Is worn to grains of drifting sand,
And angry waters foam and drift
  Through wonderous wall not made by hand.

And man looks back through time unknown
   To date the wonderous streamlet hand,
Which sculptured chasm wall of stone,
   And wore its chips to grains of sand.

But could the work a life had done
   Be seen by eyes of mortal man,
The sands that crumble one by one
   Could equal not the busy hand.

Though life is short, man leaves the stage,
   As though his wonderous work was done,
Another man, another age,
   Proves that his work has just begun.

So like the mystic cataract stream
   Which flows a myriad years through sand,
The world's adrift by light and stream,
   The work of ages, brain and hand.

The Man Who Never Stops to Think.

The man who never stops to think
    Nor count the valued time that's lost,
Oft chews tobacco, smokes or drinks,
    Regardless of result or cost.

The man who never stops to think
    Just how to manage business best,
Rush heedless down the ruinous brink
    Of bankruptcy and unsuccess.

The man who never stops to think
    How much he spends or what he makes,
Is apt to make a gradual sink
    Down, drifting to a ruinous break.

The man who never stops to think
    That educated men must work,
Is wasting time with all fools in
    Just learning how with ease to clerk.

A Lesson.

A lesson might be learned from word:
A large, fine steer within my herd
Stands near the stack, and never bawls,
But watch the fork when first it falls.
He stands by the first bunch of hay,
While others hook around and play;
He never runs and tramps around,
And tramps the hay in muddy ground;
He eats while others run and bawl,
And seeks for bunches not so small.
He's always fat, smooth, sleek and round,
While others lank would seem unsound.
A lesson here there is no doubt,
If you will try to find it out.

MRS. JOSIE B. TAYLOR.

The Bride's Farewell.

[Dedicated to my daughter, Mrs. Josie B. Taylor.]

Fare thee well, my dearest mother,
  Love's strange fancy bids me go ;
Sad to leave thee for another,
  Yet I could not answer no.
Friends most dear now linger 'round me,
  Oh! this pain words cannot tell ;
Childhood's home, how dear I love thee,
  Yet I bid thee all farewell.

Kindred friends and friends of childhood,
  And the scenes I loved so well,
Cluster 'round me like the wildwood
  Fringing 'round the little dell.
Golden forest of the highland,
  Spring time birds with thrilling song,
Bold rushing stream o'er bars and sand,
  Cheered my life when years seemed long.

The landscape painting 'gainst the wall,
  Beneath the frescoed ceiling,
Which made impressions while yet small,
  Before my eyes are stealing.

Yet I must leave thee, and forever,
　　Trust myself to another's care,
Yet our hearts we cannot sever,
　　I shall ever love thee dear.

Then, dear mother, will you miss me,
　　When the well known lamps are lit,
And will you wait for me at tea
　　When the table chairs are set?
Though I shall not hear thy sweet voice,
　　While with new friends I may roam,
Yet shall be happy with my choice,
　　And wish for thee at my home.

Mammoth Cave.

Beneath the rock, dark as the grave,
    Where endless rivers flow,
Kentucky boasts the Mammoth Cave,
    And waters pure as snow.

No eye hath seen its fountain rise,
    Yet fish swim in the stream—
But destitute are they of eyes,
    For light hath never gleamed.

It is a world within a world,
    And who can tell how vast;
Twelve miles exploring crews unfurled
    Their banner in the past.

A voice of many waters speak
    Of danger 'neath the walls,
And further man would fear to seek,
    'Mid caves and roaring falls.

What style of man beyond the shore
    Of that dark, raging stream,
Is for the Fairies to explore,
    And paint in golden dream.

15

𝕯𝖓𝖈𝖑𝖊 𝕾𝖆𝖒.

Now, Uncle Sam a bride he took,
　To represent his wealth and pride;
She turns the pages of his book,
　And finds no nation by his side.

She stands arrayed in bridal robe,
　The style of crown she there would bring,
She looks out over all the globe,
　And plucks a quill from eagle's wing.

She looks above our nation's head,
　The nation's emblem there unfurled;
She read the lines—blue, white and red—
　The proudest nation of the world.

The Goddess standing by her side
　Sends light of freedom o'er the world;
She looks away across the tide,
　To bless the flag that France unfurled.

And so they standeth, three in one,
　Representing power, wealth and fame,
To hold the Union as begun,
　But adding fuel to the flame.

Old England's envy liveth long,
   And Uncle Sam doth know it well;
He stands with seventy millions strong,
   Her useless noise and boasts to quell.

The Lion stands on England's shore,
   Growling at the American Bear;
The Bear fears not his hideous roar,
   While Stars and Stripes float in the air.

South Carolina's First Ball.

At Washington, in Relic Hall.
  Amid the relics quaint and old,
We saw Carolina's challenge ball,
  Which set the war train, death, to roll.

Two balls flew from two warriors' guns—
  One from the Gray, one from the Blue—
Met in the air, weld into one,
  Symboling North and South anew.

The Awakening of the Soul.

[Presented to Rev. J. L. Hoffman, A. M.]

The silvery dew-drops kissed the rose,
 Then slyly steals within its fold,
To wake it from its sweet repose,
 And variegate with rain-bow gold.

The voice of conscience, ever still,
 Yet whispers to the sin-dark soul;
The soul awake, with love is filled,
 And heavenly pages unfold.

The germ which seemingly was dead,
 . Like rose-buds, which the dew-drops kiss,
Awakes to feed on living bread
 And drink the wine of heavenly bliss.

Had I the oratorical powers of a Webster, and the genius of a Shakespeare, I could never paint the scene nor describe the sweet and charming ring of the song, as it appeared in this wonderful dream.   It was simply beyond all human imagination.

Strange, But True.

[Presented to Prof. Rufus Holden.]

Once in the silent shades of dream,
   I saw a strange but glorious sight:
A silvery cloud hung in a gleam,
   The heavens burnt with golden light.

The cloud moved slowly in the sky,
   But grading down, adown it came;
A moment then, and stopped on high,
   And disappeared like blown-out flame.

It left a troop on angel wings,
   Who, like a cloud, slight seemed to rise;
They tuned their silvery tongues to sing,
   While floating through the golden skies:

"I will arise and go to Jesus;
   He will embrace me in His arms;

In the arms of my dear Saviour,
    Oh! there are ten thousand charms."

Oh! Lord, that I could sing that song;
    That men of earth might hear the sound
As it reached from that throng,
    While up they rose and circled around.

Their song is one we know so well,
    And often sung at church by choir,
When new-born souls their glory tell,
    As light gleams from the heavenly fire.

Their song grew loud, and louder still;
    My soul was charmed with sound and sight;
Their golden wings, slight moved at will,
    Their brightness burnt the shades of night.

Then round and round, away on high,
    Their song grew faint, but sweeter still;
They climbed the stairway of the sky,
    To reach bright heaven's golden hill.

Their forms grew small, and smaller still;
    Their song stopped with a bell-ring tone;
They lit upon the golden hill,
    Where silvery streets lead to the throne.

Then of this vision all was gone;
    The heavens closed the golden light;

Yet, tranquilly, the song went on,
    Through happy slumbers of the night.

I saw no more, but heard the ring,
    And many days and weeks passed by,
And still I heard the angels sing
    Behind that painting in the sky.

My Own Bronzy Dear.

Let me go, let me go,
  To my own native home,
Where the light bark we row,
  And the wild forest roam.

Where my own Bronzy, dear,
  And our papoosey, Blone,
Watch and wait for my care,
  Or they die there alone.

There the bright, shiny moon
  Through the forest so deep,
Sends the bears and the 'coon
  To our field while we sleep.

And my own Bronzy, dear,
  Has no strength for the bow,
The wild varmints to clear,
  So, dear braves, let me go.

There the beautiful stream
  Flows through the wild glen,
And the theme of our dream,
  No harm the pale-faced men.

But we show friendly face,
   And we treat white man kind,
And we go to the place
   Where the game they do find.

And my own Bronzy, dear,
   With a heart pure as snow,
Drops for them friendly tear,
   So white braves, let me go.

Go thy way, red man's son,
   Seek thy own Bronzy, dear,
And with thee take my gun,
   The wild varmints to clear.

Rosy Hill.

Love thoughts come stealing o'er my brain,
  As dreams run back to youthful days,
And wish to live life o'er again,
  'Mid lovely scenes so far away.

'Mid rolling fields and widening plain,
  And golden forest fringed with pine,
Near Rosy Hill there I'd remain,
  And that dear Forest should be mine.

I loved those shades, I loved those plains;
  I loved that grove above the mill;
I loved the pines arching the lanes,
  But most of all loved Rosy Hill.

There was a-bloom a sweet bower Rose,
  And of the form there was no ill;
The son there set, the son there rose,
  For that fair Rose bloomed on a Hill.

And this fair Hill was just at home,
  Beyond the plain, with forest deep,
Where moonbeams lit the path we roamed,
  When ghostly shadows seemed to creep.

The rising son there kissed the Rose,
   And Rosy blushed like burnished gold,
And then a hue of sweet repose
   Told more than shades or blush unfold.

Ohio boasts of widening plains,
   Of rivers bold and sites to build;
But of them all, it still remains
   That I preferred the Rosy Hill.

I rambled o'er the mighty plain,
   With swamp and bog and rippling rill;
West Virginia stealing o'er my brain,
   I'd risk my life to gain a Hill.

To Mrs. J. Hamilton,

[Maysville, Kentucky.]

This mirrored shadow in the frame,
  A faint resemblance of thy charm,
When beauty won for thee a name,
  Unstained by fault, unstained by harm.

Thy youthful bloom, expression sweet,
  A loving glance from lovely eyes,
Still bears a charm for those they meet,
  Which from pure innocence can rise.

Oh, happy man who shares thy love,
  And blessed be thy daughters still,
Who seek the power from above,
  To love thee more and do thy will.

And blessed be thine only son,
  Whose business life just now is new;
Long may his prosperous business run,
  And live for self, but more for you.

Oh, lovely scenes so far away,
  When you and I were scarce nineteen,

The pleasures of that youthful day
   Have lived like shades of evergreen.

The years have dropped like golden sands,
   And left their trail of silvery gray,
Yet severs not the golden band
   Of kindred love in youthful day.

One Hundred Years Ago.

'Tis but one hundred years ago
 Since daring white men sought this land;
Then here was found the buffalo,
 And savage Indian bands.
The forest drooped o'er winding streams,
 The lonesome woods were calm and still,
Presenting but a lifeless dream,
 Beyond the eyes of skill.

The hills were clad with giant oaks,
 The lovely vales were draped in bloom,
When white man's gun the silence broke
 Amid the heathen's home.
The red man showed a friendly face,
 And pledged his honor to be true,
But, like the honor of his race,
 His pledge too soon was due.

No mercy shown to prisoners then,
 No army stood to face the foe,
But forts were built, thus to defend
 Them, ninety years ago.
The Indian warrior scaled these vales,
 They trailed our hunters in the snow,

And now we tell the warrior's tale
  Of ninety years ago.

The years have dropped like golden sands,
  And every day brought something new,
Till light of men throughout the land,
  Gleams through the nightly dew.
The world is hooped with lightning wire,
  The rivers flow above the rail,
The mountain swallows steam and fire,
  And trains sweep on the rail.

The white man's axe has swept the hills,
  And towns have grown within the vale;
The mountain streams are lined with mills,
  The world's adrift with mail.
The Indian warriors westward drift,
  Like mist before the rising sun,
Their puny arm once more they lift,
  Ere long their race is run.

Niagara.

I stood upon the wond'rous shore,
  Where foaming billows racing roll,
And muffled thunder loudly pour
  From out the current gorge of old.
The raging river down the steep,
  Rolling, foaming, roaring, boiling,
And thence to take the mighty leap,
  Plunging down in mist recoiling.

Canadian plains seem far away,
  The Cliftain House stood grand and bold,
The sun closed down on Canada
  With streaks of light and burnished gold.
We climbed the winding time-worn tower,
  Which rose above the misty falls,
Where rolling sheets with endless power
  Leap from the wond'rous curving walls.

A ship-of-war there made a leap,
  Down, plunging like a spear of steel,
Which could not rise from out the deep,
  The depths of wonder to reveal.
Some flimsy splinters, brown, and green,
  Rose to the surface with the foam,

16

And of the wreck that's all was seen
   Of what was once a warrior's home.

There red men offered sacrifice,
   And lots were cast among the girls,
And fringy wreaths and flowers nice,
   Placed in her boat to leave the world.
It fell upon the chieftain's child,
   And she the last of all his race ;
She took her seat 'mid flowers wild,
   While tears stole down the chieftain's face.

Her boat was pushed from off the shore,
   'Mid Indian screams and cheering loud,
The chief then lit a boat with oar,
   And like a streak the current plowed,
He reached his child above the fall,
   And there each other they embraced,
Then waved farewell to one and all,
   While tears stole down each bronzy face.

Yet they believed a hunting ground
   Was in the golden far away,
Where blooming forests ere abound,
   And time is but an endless day.
Each year they sent their proxy on,
   A blooming girl and boat of flowers,
And worshipped at the early dawn,
   The symbol falls with endless powers.

Kiss Her, Quick, You Little Goose.

At sight I loved Miss Nellie dear,
 And Polly parrot loved her, too,
I courted both for one long year,
 And Polly, too, was ever true.
She said one day: "I is your friend,
 And Nellie, dear, does love you, too."
So first and last, and to the end,
 Miss Polly's chat was ever new.

She watched us close, she'd steal our words,
 And tell them to a laughing crowd;
Yet I to others much preferred;
 And of her Nellie ever proud.
My timid soul more timid grew,
 And oh! I loved Miss Nellie dear;
But, then, if Polly only knew,
 She'd surely tell it everywhere.

The train I rode went half-past nine;
 When parting, oft I wished to say:
"Oh! Nellie, dear, wilt thou be mine?"
 But there was Polly in the way.
The last of June, a lovely day,
 The summer-house was sweet with bloom;

There we, as lovers, hid away—
  Left busy Polly in the room.

But Polly stole within a fold,
  And perched on trellis over-head,
With eyes set in two rings of gold,
  And no deaf ear to what was said.
Still as the ghost of thistle flowers,
  Our strutting little Polly stood,
And caught each sacred word of ours,
  And all our secrets understood.

The hour drew near "the parting nine,"
  My stammering tongue refused to go;
At last I said: "Wilt thou be mine?"
  "Oh, sir, I cannot answer no."
" Kiss her, kiss her, quick, you little goose!"
  I kissed her, quick, the clock struck nine,
And then my stammering tongue was loose,
  And Nellie, dear, was ever mine.

Result of Thought.

[Dedicated to My Brother-in-Law, Hon. Valentine Langfitte.]

Two bright-eyed boys were sent to school
　Through all their happy youthful days;
Were governed by the golden rule
　At home, in school, and in their plays.
Their kingly mansion, near a town,
　Looked out upon a crystal stream,
Which coursed its banks, the eastern bounds
　Of mills their father ran by steam.

The fringe of wealth hung at the door,
　And two bright boys alone to train,
The craving heart could ask no more
　In point of wealth and earthly gain;
So wealth and pride great efforts made
　To train these boys for wealth and fame,
And parents sought wise teachers' aid,
　Whose merits won for them a name.

These twins, now sixteen summers'·old,
　Sat by their blazing, cozy fire;
One talked and dwelt on themes of gold,
　The other sought a station higher;

One spoke of gold behind the bar,
    And rich hotels in city style,
The other spoke of church and choir,
    Renouncing evil all the while.

They both grew up bright, happy men,
    Each launched his boat upon life's sea;
One took the Bible and the pen,
    The other took the hotel key.
For one had watched the parson well,
    Who always dwelt on truth and fame;
The other's pride was the hotel,
    Where devils booked the drunkard's name.

One preached of Christ, the heavenly star,
    And pressed his claims upon the soul;
The other stood behind the bar,
    To barter life and soul for gold.
He painted charms upon the wall;
    He lit his house with brilliant lights;
A cordial welcome, one and all,
    To come and spend the pleasant nights.

His bar was on the gilt-edge style,
    His billiard-room was fringed with gold,
His card-room open all the while,
    The young and giddy there to mould.
His house became an evil den,
    His family drifted with its charms,

His death was at a tremor's end,
  His wealth was wrecked as by a storm.

His brother, now a parson gray,
  Stands firm as in the days of youth;
His course is marked with grand display
  Of ministerial love and truth.
His life is one continual ray
  Of brilliant gleamings from the throne,
And souls that live in endless day
  Will wear the crown of seed there sown.

Two flowers standing side by side,
  Each envious of the other's bloom,
Day after day still grew their pride,
  Till both were changed and they were one.
So thought and pride youth's bloom will guide,
  To variegate with good or ill,
And should one choose the evil side,
  The heart is taught to love it still.

'Tis thought that makes a man a name,
  No lazy brain can ever gain
Great honors, wealth or scuptured fame,
  He merely drags a life in vain.
Minds deep and great, great deeds have done
  To scan mysterious worlds on high,
While thoughtless men their course have run,
  Like thistle blossoms in the sky.

Thought is the keystone in the arch
    Which spans the door to sculptured fame;
There Morse and Fulton led the march,
    Their steam and lightning to proclaim.
Now Edison speaks across the land,
    And Morse has laid the ocean wire,
And Fulton placed in mortal hand
    The blaze which set the world on fire.

Scenes of Childhood.

[Dedicated to My Brother, Mr. C. G. Davis, and Elizabeth, His Wife.]

Oh, the long, long, dear long ago,
Fifty years or more, I know,
When I a child at mother's knee
Could read the love she had for me.
She stamped her image on my heart
And bid its charms ne'er to depart;
Her voice was music, soft and sweet,
Stood slightly tall, handsome and neat.

Oft' she sat by the spinning wheel,
Spinning threads for the noiseless reel,
Drawing flax from the distaff rest,
Wound in shape of a hornet's nest.
She spun the long rolls made of wool,
And wound the large spools round and full,
To feed the brown old-fashioned loom,
Which stood just in another room.

Then sister wove the whole day long,
And trained her voice with lover's song;
And little sister wound the quill,
And we repaired the flutter mill,

And built a dam across the stream,
To use its power in place of steam:
But when complete, though strong and neat,
We had no burrs to grind the wheat.

But. like the noiseless spinner's reel,
The mill consisted of a wheel,
Which threw its rolling silvery spray
In rainbow mist of grand display.
The mill was all we claimed for it.
But was not worth a phip'ny-bit,
So then we left the worthless mill,
And went out slightly on the hill.

And there we cleared a little field,
Small timbers fell'd, the large ones peeled,
And dug the ground for early corn,
And planted it one bright Spring morn.
The ground squirrel took a little scout,
And found the seed that we put out ;
He knew I was too small to shoot,
He dug my corn out by the root.

Then, like an ape, sat on his heel,
And of my corn would make a meal;
This raised my boy ambition high,
And then I planned that he should die :
I made wood triggers. neat and small,
And set the well-known trap, " dead fall,"

And then again in early morn
He came to steal the trigger-corn.

But when he bit the trigger-thread,
The trap-stone fell and he was dead;
The corn was saved, the victory won,
And thus a farmer boy begun.
And then away to valley field,
With timbers dead and partly peeled,
To heap dry logs upon the ground,
And burn dead limbs that crumbled down.

A cloud of smoke hung o'er the farm,
The scenes of which a lasting charm
Has followed to this distant day,
Of care-worn head and silvery gray.
Then boys and father tilling corn,
Awaited calls of dinner horn;
There wigeons pecked the dotted tree,
And built a nest no one could see.

They plucked the corn to feed their young,
And paid their bills with songs they sung;
The wood-peck thief, with blood-red head,
Also in fields with timber dead,
Would pluck the corn the whole day long,
And then go home without a song;
When evening shades were growing long,
Swamp robin, in a happy song,

Oft' touched the sweetest chord e'er heard
From any charming forest bird.
His home was in the forest green,
His golden plumage seldom seen,
But champion of the world in song,
He raised his voice so shrill and strong
It touched the valley hills around,
And echoed back the charming sound.

Those charming birds and lovely scene
All disappeared with Summer green;
Then golden forest leaves came down,
And covered all the woodland ground,
And often came the dread alarm,
Of fence in danger round the farm;
Hark! Hark! the woodland warning fire!
'Tis sweeping fast and flaming higher.

In angry flames it climbs the trees,
And rides in wrath on every breeze;
It leaps across the ravine wall,
Dead timbers piecemeal reel and fall;
It climbs the mountain like a steed,
And sweeps through woods tornado speed,
The fox and deer fly from the flame,
Fly, swiftly fly, all kinds of game.

The smoke and flame have raised alarm,
And neighbors rushing to the farm,

Rake fast, and fire around the field,
The fence if possible to shield.
The smoke rolls up in fleecy train,
The sun shines on, but all in vain,
The scene is but a smoky world,
Which wraps itself in silvery pearl.

The sun moves slowly through the sky,
With deep red veil hung o'er his eye;
The silken curtain of the night
Close moon and stars all out of sight;
The morning sun o'er mountains high,
A blood-red painting in the sky,
Moves all day long and passes by,
But minus power to dim the eye.

Now after many years away,
I sought the home of childhood's day;
But, oh! a sad and wond'rous change—
'Twas not my home, it all looked strange.
A kingly throne with golden dome,
Could not be valued with my home;
I wished no change, however grand,
I wished no change in forest land.

But wished it like the days of old,
When forest draped in wreaths of gold;
I missed each bush and every tree,
O'er farm and hills so dear to me;

Each carried sadness with its loss,
And changes grand were only dross,
The two grand oaks upon the hill,
Were slain by axe and hauled to mill.

The ground which once had claimed the barn,
Was plowed and planted now in corn;
The sweep was torn down from the well,
By windlass rope the bucket fell.
The moss-grown walls were worn by time,
Which formed slight steps I used to climb
To wash and clean the bottom stone,
Where nature's fountain held its own.

The old-time house was torn away,
A new one made a grand display,
With finished halls and stylish rooms;
But oh, alas! 'twas not my home.
The rudest block in old-time walls,
More dearly prized than rooms and halls;
Its walls were built of axe-hewn wood,
Storm-proof, in forest lands it stood,

To welcome hunter, brave and true,
When inmates numbered only two;
There first the muffled axe was heard,
Which startled all the native herd
That roamed those hills and forest vale,
And left the only dingy trail.

There stood those walls mid fields of green,
When family numbered just fourteen.

There stood those walls when all were gone,
And no one prized its door as home ;
Yet memories dear lived in the breast
Of those whom that dear home had blest,
And for its loss a tear was shed,
Deep as the wails o'er loved ones dead ;
The rippling brook from nearest hill,
Where dams were made for flutter mill,

Was forced from nature's winding wall
Through home-made channels deep and small,
And not a bank nor e'en a trace
Was left to mark its rightful place.
The cabin cribs were both torn down,
And not a trace left on the ground ;
The creek had worn its banks away—
A wond'rous change since boyhood day.

The woodland grove just near my home,
Where pheasant beats his muffled drum,
Was swept away, and now the quail
Was monarch of that little vale.
The highland peaks near home all 'round,
Where golden forests once abound,
Were stripped of all that grand display
Which charmed my heart in childhood day.

My home bird's gone to distant hills,
To blend their songs with whip-poor-wills,
And sing for settlers of the woods,
The forest wilds of my boyhood.
But now a hundred cottage homes
Are planted where I used to roam,
O'er lovely forest hills and vales,
A wood for deer and varmint trails.

The wildwood land, home of the owl,
Where wolf sneaked off with hideous howl,
And panther slept on bended trees,
Is now the happy home of ease.
The old school-house is torn away,
Ground sodded green once worn by play,
Where game ran high by swift moved feet,
And battle raged, fear of defeat.

A thought came o'er me with a tear—
This sodded play-ground, once so dear,
Asked me the question sad and deep:
How many of your playmates sleep
Beneath a sod like this of mine?
The answer of; ten, perhaps nine.
The new school-house of rustic wood,
A ragged beggar quaintly stood,

With moss-grown logs o'er window small,
And birds had built upon the wall,

The desk and seats had crumbled down,
The floor lay mouldering on the ground,
The rude stone chimney, lank and tall,
Was bending from the school-house wall,
And ruin hung o'er all the scene,
Where old-time school was ever green.

The hills seemed tall and far away,
Long mountain shades at close of day;
Green waving fields of grass and rye,
Where forest peaks once propped the sky.
The valleys spread their blue grass wings,
The little brooks were fed by springs;
The windings of the well-known stream,
Were lost in grassy fields of green.

The rolling fields of golden grain,
Like sea waves drifting in a train,
Rolled o'er the hills and mountains high,
Recoiling 'gainst the rosy sky,
The sun went down o'er fields of grain,
Which spread o'er hilltops and the plain,
Where unmolested forest stood,
When father felled the first wildwood.

His axe was first in all the plain,
His gun was first the wood to stain,
His rooster blew the first shrill horn
To warn the forest herds of morn.

17

All sounds were muffled by the trees,
And slightly stirred the forest breeze.
Sketched from those scenes of forest gloom,
You have the painting of my home.

The Sunset of Life.

The silvery cords of life are winding
   Around the rolling beams of time;
Life's sun, reflecting while declining,
   Bright gilds the dreamy shades of rhyme.

To distant worlds in the flight of dream
   On swift wings of the soul we ride,
Where the planet, stars and soft moon-beam,
   Through ethereal deep seem to glide.

Bright seas beyond that mystic shore,
   Where mysterious transports sweep,
And the art of man can ne'er explore,
   Lie smouldering in the starry deep.

Worlds half hidden by the veil of time,
   In their refulgent grandeur roll,
To tempt the venturous pen of rhyme
   Their wonderous beauty to unfold.

Thus golden sheaves from our sickle fall;
   Imaginary fields stretch far away;
Life's sun hangs o'er its mountains tall;
   The shadows fall to close the day.

Silken Thread.

Two hills of corn stood in the field,
And as the shoots rose for the yield,
From out the shoots soft silken thread
Thus to its near-by neighbor said:
"Now could my bloom meet silk of thine,
'Twould then be sure the bloom of mine."
And thus arranged, the trade was made,
And each one gave the other aid.
Now when the farmer to the field
Came for the stalks and for the yield,
The farmer to his servant said:
"This hill is white and this one red."
Each took his hill back to the bin,
The husk removed and there within
Were grains of white and grains of red.
The farmer to his servant said:
"The bloom from off the tassel head,
Has fell upon the silken thread."
The bloom of youth with silken thread,
From evil stocks are often fed,
The husk may hide, but there within
Are grains of innocence stained with sin.

Recruiting for the Lord.

We are now recruiting for the Lord,
  The gospel drum rings clear and strong,
Eternal joy, the great reward,
  For all who join our happy throng.

We'r moving on the train of time,
  It cannot stop, it cannot slack;
Our camp is in a world sublime,
  Once there we never shall come back.

We'r fighting for the great reward,
  For that dear land beyond the skies,
Where angels sing and praise the Lord,
  And pleasure never, never dies.

Fall in before the roll is call'd,
  The train is sweeping o'er the plain,
The drum rings loud for one and all,
  If Heaven is lost, Hell must be gain'd.

A branch road, and it is known well,
  The track is broad, the way is clear,
Eternal fire in pits of Hell,
  Reward of those who muster there.

Large bounty and a crown for all,
  Who step time with the gospel drum,
Our flag-staff rests on Heaven's wall,
  Who will enlist? Oh! who will come?

Army of the Dragon.

I dream'd of Satan and his clan,
  Who came to earth at dead of night,
Satan with horns leading the van,
  With martial tramp and quick of flight.

And as he marched at this dread hour,
  He changed from devil to a queen,
With beauty charming and with power,
  Changing all to a lovely scene.

The fairest of the earthly fair,
  The fairest damsel with her charm,
To his fair face could not compare,
  Nor stand so distant from all harm.

To see him was to look and love,
  Lose sight of hellish scenes before,
Admire him as one from above,
  Even the God we all adore.

Just then appeared a rushing throng,
  Half-human, with satanic gaze,
All quick as flash, with movements strong,
  A flash of light, and then a blaze.

Speechless they tramped, as armies swelled,
  Their fife and bugle gave no sound,

Bands with their silent drums of Hell,
  Stepped time that seem'd to jar the ground.

Satan appeared in all his might
  With flaming eyes and shining horns,
A flash of day, a flash of night,
  His devils wearing crowns of thorns.

Horrors of Hell came thick and fast,
  My soul was chill'd with deathly dread,
I could not see the first nor last,
  As spirits dam'd still onward sped.

The silence broke, by battle-fire,
  A jarring tramp, a war-like sound,
Music from Hell's invented lyre,
  And drums that seem'd to jar the ground.

Discordant sounds of music swell'd,
  A storming fire of grape and shell,
From guns cast in the pits of Hell,
  Where the Devil and his angels fell.

Earth trembled, the waters quivered,
  And the strongest buildings rattled,
And bravest men stood back and shivered,
  As though Hell rose 'gainst earth in battle.

Why we dream, may be hard to tell,
  But stranger still, such dreams of Hell.
This is no fiction.

A Speech by Col. D. H. Davis, July 4, 1878.

Ladies and Gentlemen:

Through the providence of Almighty God, we this day have the privilege of meeting in this beautiful grove to celebrate this great day, in memory of the events of our nation's birth.

One hundred and two years ago this day, the Declaration of the Independence of these United States was signed by the heroes of seventeen hundred and seventy-six, and proclaimed to the world.

The astonished nations, startled as though they had just awoke from a long slumber, when they read in that declaration that all men were created equal and should have equal rights.

This new idea of equal rights and liberty inspired the down trodden people of the colonies with new energies to push forward with the death-pealing thunders of war, in hope of securing to our beloved country peace and liberty. From that day the words freedom and liberty have ever been music to every true American heart.

When we look back through the pages of history, and view our beloved country in her death struggle for liberty, with her thirteen colonies and about four millions of people, and contrast the condition of our country then with

18

the present, we can scarcely realize that such a wonderful change could have taken place in so short a time.

The State of New York alone to-day outnumbers the whole of the thirteen colonies at the close of the Revolutionary War. We have grown up from a mere child, as it were, to manhood in stature, to a mighty power in strength, and, to the world's great astonishment, in skill and wealth. We have surpassed all other nations in gigantic business-houses and manufactures, and have a controlling influence over the nations of the earth in point of wealth and agricultural productions. Large towns and cities have sprung up from East to West and from North to South ; and, to-day is heard the rumbling sound of the iron horse from the Pacific to the Atlantic Ocean. The once dreary home of the savage is now the home of intelligence and religious liberty.

The wide spreading plains of the Western prairie are to-day loaded with their fields of golden grain. Our country is checkered with railroads. Our lakes and rivers are noisy with steam; and our beautiful valleys are dotted with towns, churches and school-houses. The gigantic oaks, which once so thickly clustered over these hills and vales, long since have bowed to the earth, and we to-day are surrounded by these beautiful fields of green ; these lovely homes and sparkling eyes of intelligence, with the old star-spangled banner floating above our nation's head, which guarantees to every American citizen the right to worship God according to the dictates of their own conscience, under their own vine and fig tree, where none dare to molest or make them afraid. The sons of the red man, much against their will, long since surrendered these hills to the white man's axe ; and while we are blessed with all the bounties of life, their wigwams may be found in the farthest plains of the West, near the snow-capped peaks of the Rocky Mountains.

And though we have grown up to a mighty power in strength and perhaps have surpassed all other nations in point of wealth, yet, according to our statistics, the entire wealth of the United States is increasing at the rate of about one hundred per cent. in ten years. We have grown up from a population of about four millions to a population of more than forty millions, and yet, we as a nation, are just in our infancy. But, with our mighty lakes and rivers, our railroads and canals, our rich and fertile soil, our extensive territories of the West, and our vast mineral resources, we are destined at no distant day to become one of the most powerful and wealthy nations on the face of the globe. For all these blessings of liberty and wealth we are indebted to the heroes of seventeen hundred and seventy-six ; to the signers of the Declaration of our Independence ; to the brave warriors who laid down their life for our freedom, and to the noble Washington and Lafayette who planned our battles and who rolled on and on the charriot-wheels of victory until the mighty demon of war was compelled to abandon the American soil ; while a triumphant shout went up from every true American heart, and the old star-spangled banner, for the first time, gently floated in the heavenly breeze of peace and liberty.

www.ingramcontent.com/pod-product-compliance
Lightning Source LLC
Chambersburg PA
CBHW020347030726
47496CB00007B/2035